Dream of the Spirit Man

A NOVEL BY GEORGE MENDOZA

WISE TREE PRESS
Mesilla Park, New Mexico

Published by Wise Tree Press.

Wise Tree Press is an imprint of the
Wise Tree Foundation, INC.
P.O. Box 1243, Mesilla Park, New Mexico 88047.

www.georgemendoza.com

Library of Congress Control Number: 9798985883848

To my daughter,

Maria G. Mendoza

Author's Note

In 2011, I had a terrible hiking accident in the Organ Mountains of New Mexico, where I live and dream my dreams. I fell a good thirty feet, breaking my arm and my teeth. I suffered from cluster headaches for a long time after that fall.

The headaches and pain led to a wildly productive period during which I painted up a storm and wrote novels about my superhero, the Spirit Man. Vivid visions danced behind my eyelids, and the strokes of my brush and my pen recreated those beautiful images, turning them into this story.

Then, one day, the headaches stopped, but I continued to paint and write books. I guess it's true that a good bump on the head can bring out creativity! I have been accused of living in a fantasy and dreaming my life away. That's probably true, and I would not have it any other way.

Dream of the Spirit Man is the fourth book in the series, following *Journey of the Spirit Man*, *Vision of the Spirit Man*, and *Heart of the Spirit Man*.

Acknowledgements

I would like to express my appreciation to Erne Barge, Dr. David Boje, Mindy Byrnes, Louie Burke, and Rachel Carrillo; to the Castillo family; to my art teacher, Imelda Chacon; to Bobby Cook and Mayra Enriquez; to my sister Kathleen Firth, Dick Guttman, Janus Herrera, Jennifer Romero, and Neal Hidalgo; to Anne Hillerman, Craig Holden, Dr. Dan Howard, Sonny Irizarry, Thomas Kindig, and Doylene Land; to Daniel Landes, Jamie Lapage, James McConnell, and Michael Marrufo; to my son, Michael Mendoza; to J.L. Powers, Robert Rivera, Ron Rowlett and his son, Ryan Rowlett; to Antonio Sanchez, Jane Seymour, Mary Sherman, Holly Watson, and Thomas Zubia; and to all the others who wish to remain anonymous.

I am very grateful to James Salas and Raquel Ortega with the New Mexico Commission for the Blind, who funded this incredible book project; to Jessica Powers and Kathy McInnis, who designed this beautiful book; to my agent, Frank Weimann, Folio Literary Management, New York; and to my creative editor, Ericka Jordan, the Spirit Woman with the magic touch!

— continued —

I give special thanks to New Mexico State University, the NMSU English Department, and especially the Creative Writing staff for their help and support in this and other projects.

All characters in this book are figments of my imagination with the exception of Michael Spirit Man.

.

George Mendoza
New Mexico

Chapter 1

Michael was stuck in the throes of a nightmare unlike any he had known.

Desperate for escape from the hellish place he found himself in now, Michael felt around the darkness that enveloped him, feeling the cold grooves of brick beneath the tips of his fingers. With a short, self-assured nod, Michael dragged himself to his feet and broke out into a sprint, running like the wind itself; he was running toward a speck of light in the far distance that soon burst into a wall of tall flames. Fire surrounded him on every side. In fact, the world was burning up in a living hell. Hope was fading away, hell, hope was long gone. The world had fallen into a state so cold and unfamiliar, so filled with greed, war, corruption, and murder, that Michael feared he might never recognize it again; but what could one person do to stop what seemed to be inevitable?

The dream ended; or maybe not.

Michael was back home now, back in New Mexico at his estate, Spirit Land. The relief he felt was short lived, soon replaced by a sense of loneliness as he recalled his solitude in the vastness of the home. Sure, living in a secluded mansion had its perks. The chance of solicitors bothering him as he went about his day-to-day life was low, but so were the chances of receiving other visitors. It was lonely.

Michael woke up to a world of chaos and madness. The world was spiraling. And in a way, so was he—and there was nothing he could do about it. The powerlessness of it all kept striking him, so often that it almost felt like he might as well lie down and die.

Of course, the thought of dying seemed silly. He had died so many times before. What was death but something to come back from? It was an inconvenience, nothing more. Something that he overcame, like everything else he'd encountered in his many travels.

Michael looked in a mirror, studying his face. It hadn't changed one bit in the last several years. He looked the same as he did when he was twenty-three and not one day older. He was immortal. That was the true nature of the Spirit Man. Kill the body, but the spirit comes back to life over and over again. Break his body then watch his spirit wake his very soul.

Michael felt at the paper cut on his thumb, absentmindedly pressing on it. Even though it was a little cut he could barely feel, it still brought back memories of his struggles in all the worlds he had visited. Pain, pleasure. Darkness, light. Hate, love. War, peace. There was a fine line between all these strange forces in the human experience, and he felt all of them. The human world was slipping into chaos and senseless violence and madness and everyone was killing each other for the sport of it. It was the eve of destruction and the end of days. Michael could feel it in his bones. The Spirit Man wanted to change the world, but he knew he couldn't save it from itself.

He still had dreams for the future, and no matter what struggles come your way, you must keep your dream alive. All ten million of them. You have to be brave, be strong.

He closed his eyes, safe in his home in Spirit land, and tried to send his mind out into the ravaged world, trying to find answers. Letting himself relax in the comfort of his chair, he tried to access other senses, other visions, other places that might be able to give him some insight into the path ahead of him.

The wind blew hotter and harder over the west mesa in New Mexico. Michael sat on top of a rock in the middle of the desert. In his mind's eye, he could see a gigantic bright yellow-and-red sign on the old building in Las Cruces, reading Shook Tires. "Shook," Michael whispered. Distant memories flooded his mind—of faraway lands and fantastic adventures.

One particular memory stood out, Suckfly telling him not to look for the girl with three eyes and the fabled white stone. "The white stone is a farce, stupid Spirit Man. You're wasting your time. Your

   DREAM OF THE SPIRIT MAN

world is a cesspool of grief and pain. So fucking corrupt—beyond redemption, even by my standards! Why would anyone want to save it? For what?"

For what, indeed. Even Michael had to wonder if humanity was worth saving at times, with its wars and death.

He had to wonder, did the white stone exist? Could the girl with three eyes really help the mess that they were trapped in? Did the stone have a hole in it? Was it a seeing eye? What was the name of the little girl with three eyes? She had a third eye in the middle of her forehead, so she should be easy enough to find. But where was she? Who was she to him? Was he dreaming? Was she even real?

She was wearing a dress covered in tiny mirrors, just floating above him, laughing. She carried a white stone in her right hand which had a tiny hole in it. She lifted it to her eye, peering down at Michael, before floating away, laughing like a madman all the while.

Michael woke up with a jerk. He was on the sand. Hadn't his dream started inside his home…? He couldn't be sure, now that he was awake, where he'd been before the dreaming. He could not remember any of the crazy stuff floating in his head at all. He only knew there was no time for sleeping now. There was too much work to do. Too many vision quests to ponder and act upon. Too many roads to walk down and mountains to climb up. Too many worlds to change and save. Too many better tomorrows to wish for. "I have wished and dreamed my life away, and for what?" Michael asked himself silently.

"We live, we die, and we learn our lessons along the way. By the time we learn our lessons, we might as well be dead. Our lessons learned, if any are learned at all, all become buried with us and blow away like dust in the wind. What is it all for?" he wondered aloud.

Michael looked over to his far right and saw a magical blue door with a sun painted in its upper right-hand corner. The perfect sky-blue door was suspended in midair about three to four feet above the ground.

Michael had come to this particular spot around eight o'clock in the morning in the middle of October. It was now four o'clock in the afternoon and the blue door was still hanging around like it was waiting for something dramatic to happen. The door seemed to tug at his spirit and he could feel it pulling him somehow. The blue door had a spirit of its own, somehow, though what kind of spirit a door might have was uncertain. Michael had been in this desert place for nearly eight hours, wondering what he was doing there. Nothing was clear to him in his sun-drenched mind. He sat on a flat white rock that stood about twenty-five feet away from the hovering blue door. There was a happy face painted in the middle of it. Thick black strokes of black paint made a perfect smiley face on the sun, though it looked a bit insane to the spirit man. Was the sun mocking him? What was so funny anyway? "Smile away, dude!"

Michael took a drink of water from a plastic bottle he had brought with him on his desert walk. After he drank himself silly, he shuffled his feet in the loose red and yellow sands of the New Mexican desert. The world was a sad place. There was nothing funny about living life anymore. The dark side was on the move again and Michael could feel it. He could feel the dark force growing in his heart and soul. The Visionaries would have to rise up and fight the dark side once again.

"There are too many wars," whispered the Spirit Man. "So much blood upon the lands. Death and destruction are everywhere."

His hope was fading away. Hell, hope was gone, or at least, that's what it felt like lately.

Michael shouted from deep within his soul, "Overcome we shall!"

The sky-blue spirit of the door seemed to call out to the Spirit Man, but Michael tried hard to ignore it. He knew that he could walk over to the door and go through it to the other side. He always did cross over. It was just a matter of time and that feeling was gnawing at his gut. "What's the point? It will just be full of death and destruction like every time I visit. What was it all for?"

He knew that there were many more battles to be fought and blood to be shed. He knew that dreams would be broken, lives would be lost, and tears would fall like a waterfall upon the land. He knew that the world would drown in a sea of darkness and that the three-eyed girl was their only hope. So many gods have tried to save the world, but they all failed. "Why should things be any different for me? Who am I?" Was the girl with three eyes a goddess? Could she really save the world from the eve of destruction and the so-called end of days?

Michael shook his head. He did not want to cross over again. It didn't matter what happened. He didn't know how many more journeys he had in him, and it took so much out of him to consider crossing over on half a chance, a whisper of a promise from a voice he didn't recognize. There was too much that was uncertain. Should he really bet his spirit once more on yet another journey?

The sky-blue door whispered to him, "Come on in, Michael Seymour. Come in! I have something real special just for you, oh Spirit Man."

But Michael turned his head away from the blue door in the middle of the desert. He had been out in the hot sun for too long and was beginning to feel faint, the dry heat bearing down on him like a great yellow eye glaring a hole in the back of his neck. "I have to get out of here soon," he said to himself. He then stared blankly into the nothingness for a long time.

The hot desert wind blew like a furnace across the empty desert. As the wind whipped around him, the whistle blew for the oncoming Amtrak train coming from El Paso, Texas. Michael watched with great curiosity as the train slowly passed by him in the desert. The train moved smoothly past Michael and the strange blue door. The white rock Michael was sitting on was fifty yards from the train. But no one saw him, and they did not see the magical blue door either. Michael could feel the lack of eyes on him, would have sensed if anyone looked his way. The train was a double decker and most of the windows were darkly tinted, making it difficult to see if anyone was riding it at all. In the middle of the long train, there was a lone car with clear windows in it. As it passed by Michael, he could see a small group of rowdy zombies and bat demons, partying their asses off, drinking and smoking cigars.

"Ghost train," Michael mused and then laughed in the middle of nowhere. "I must be going crazy."

Soon the train made its way across the desert and it slowly disappeared into the distant western horizon. Michael scooped up some dirt with his right hand and threw it back down onto the ground. The wind carried the fine dust up and away from him. The wind also felt hot against his face. He got up to his feet, stretched his back and shoulders, and then walked over to the blue door.

It was late October and he hated to go but he knew he had to cross over to the Other Side. It was a shame because October was his favorite month in New Mexico, and he hated to miss it. Cool mornings were perfect for a hot cup of coffee or tea and the warm afternoons were perfect for a long walk in the desert or mountains. But it was time to go and he knew it. He was feeling restless in his spirit like he wanted to go on a long vacation and get away from everyone. This restless feeling in his spirit was different this time. One long dark dream after another disturbed his sleep. He woke up in the middle of the night in a pool of sweat and sheer terror, screaming for help, but no one ever came.

So many dreams and visions. There was the haunting dream about the poisonous spider, but the poison didn't kill him. There was the strange dream about the rainbow-colored snake that crawled into his brain one night. It coiled there and hissed, but it did not strike or kill him either. The snake just crawled around in his brain and then he woke up. Snakes and spiders. His dreams were terrifying and haunting and real as hell. He longed for a good night's sleep, which escaped him. And of course, there were the nagging dreams of a huge yellow stone, a white stone, one dead Michael Seymour and the little girl with the three eyes. Damn it, what was her name? So many dreams, but did they mean anything?

It was time to cross over. It was time to go and he knew it now as the feeling pressed stronger and stronger in his guts. Michael stood in front of the blue door which was about ten feet high. The sun looked like one of the abstract suns his friend painted. George's art show had traveled to numerous art galleries and museums throughout the world and he received much acclaim. George was one of the few people who knew Michael was the Spirit Man and he liked that just fine. The fewer people that knew his true identity and his whereabouts and moves made it easier for the Spirit Man to go from one world to another without being detected or noticed or missed all that much.

Michael stood at the door for a long time, studying it. A very thin gold line framed the blue door. There was no doorknob. Only deep blueness and one insane smiley happy-faced sun in the middle of the door and the blue sky swirling around it. A bright yellow leaf fell out of the sky. It drifted down through the blue sky like a soft feather, flipping in the soft wind. Michael had no idea where it came from. There were no trees out here for miles in this empty desert world and the blue sky was a fake blue. The yellow leaf fell down by his feet. Michael bent down but decided against it. He would leave the leaf in peace as a marker of some kind.

"I wish I could just stay here like you, my golden friend. I'll see you when I get back home to New Mexico, if I can ever find my way back here. I think if I go, I might not ever come back this time. What do you think?"

The leaf didn't answer. Of course not. This was the real world, after all...right? Where the only things that talked were people, and most of the things they said were lies. Maybe it'd be better if leaves were the ones with the power to make speech. Michael's thought process was cut off, though, by the sound of a low, moaning creak, stuttering occasionally like a creaky stone fence.

The blue door had opened on its own. It was time to leave for sure.

Behind the door was a swirling mist of blues, greens, and violets. Two feminine hands reached out and grabbed Michael's shirt, yanking him inside. In a blink of an eye, he slipped from one world to another time and place. The wind blew hard across the desert and the blue door vanished, only the briefest settling of sand in the wind marking its disappearance from the world.

In the valley below and far from the west mesa, two children were playing in a small pile of raked leaves. The two children played and laughed as they jumped up and down and ran through the pile of fallen leaves. Then suddenly, a dust devil came along and blew the leaves up into the air and carried the dry leaves miles away over the desert.

The hot dry wind swept over the desert lands. Soon the sun set and night fell upon the land. And Michael was long gone, gone to a brand new world of colors and images just like a famous abstract painting.

Michael flew through a sea of kaleidoscope colors as his body spun out of control, the only constant thing the two hands gripping onto his shirt, pulling him away from the world of the real and back once more to the world of the dream, of the fantastic, of the spirit.

Michael soared like a bullet to another place and time, far away from his home in New Mexico, and as his heart pounded in his chest, he couldn't help but feel the thrill once more, deep in his bones. The excitement of the adventure, his to claim again, dragged him forward into the unknown.

Chapter 2

Michael flew past a million balls of white light. Flying past a million dying suns blinking their last as he zoomed through the air at tremendous speeds. There was so much light. So many colors. So much space and time here. Wherever here was. Michael was lost in time and space as he crossed over from one world to another place and time. Breaking daylight and a blinding flash of light and dazzling colors exploded in the back of his eyes. His body spun up and down, out of control, for a long time, until it made more sense to just close his eyes and wait for it to be over than to try to make sense of meaningless words like "up" or "down."

A second later, Michael stood in the middle of a desert again, but this desert wasn't familiar. It wasn't New Mexico at all. It felt different. Vast desert vistas revealed red and yellow sandstone formations, a blazing sun in a clear turquoise sky, and rolling brown hills with sage green bushes growing on the hillsides. White sand dunes rolled like ocean waves across the lands and beyond. Tall majestic mountains were towering in the east, but these were not the famous Organ Mountains from back home in New Mexico. Michael couldn't quite put his finger on it, but it was obvious to him that this was not any world he'd ever been to in the real world he'd once belonged to.

But one thing stood out as particularly odd. There was a massive historic wooden sign in front of him that read, "DW#15 Where dreams bloom if you make room!"

Beyond the wooden sign were six long straight lines of hundreds of blue doors, stretching away from Michael in perfect even rows. Every blue door seemed to have a painted crazy smiley sun in the upper right corner of the frame. Some of the blue doors had golden doorknobs crafted to look like tiny glowing suns. At the end of the long rows of blue doors stood three massive windmills. Their long arms spun around and around like mad machines. Huge faces superimposed themselves on the top portion of the gigantic windmills. These faces spoke to Michael, "Go away, Crap Man! Get out of here!" Their voices were high and anxious, yet somehow boomed across the distance between them and Michael as easily as if they were speaking right next to him.

Michael could not believe what he saw. He froze in place as he squinted his eyes in the bright sunlight of this strange new world that he was lost in. "Another soul lost in limbo," he mused. "Where am I this time? What is this place?"

Michael ignored the windmills and their panicked yelling and focused on the doors. He took one step forward on the soft desert sands before stopping dead in his tracks. Which door should he take? He saw the six lines of blue doors stretching for miles toward the rugged tall mountains in the east. How many doors were there? There had to be hundreds, if not a few thousand. He began to walk in the desert sands toward the blue doors. There was no clear path here. The blue door that was closest to him stood in the middle of a small hill. The door seemed to call out to him, "Come in, Spirit Man! Come in!"

Michael walked over to the door and stopped in front of it. The door shimmered in the dazzling sunlight as he stood still for a long time. In his many travels, he'd rarely regretted taking an extra few moments before choosing a path. After he took his sweet time considering the door, Michael took a few steps toward it, only to stop when the disembodied female hands appeared in front of him, waving frantically, before making an "X." He guessed he shouldn't go through that door, then, after all.

"Which door should I take then? Lead me there." He peered critically at the disembodied hands. They stopped at the wrist, reminding him of creepy creatures from bad Halloween movies, but oddly, they didn't seem frightening to him. Their fingernails were short and clean, and as they floated in the air, Michael wondered how he knew for sure that they were a woman's hands.... Really, he had no more reason to trust this floating pair of hands than he did to trust the blue doors themselves. But the hands had brought him into this world, so he supposed he might as well let them grab the reins for a while. "So? If you're going to help me, then help me figure out where I'm supposed to go from here, huh?"

The hands gave him a thumb's up and flew away, Michael fast on their heels... If a pair of hands could even have heels, that is. He walked for miles, sun beating down on his head like fire coming from hell itself. He had no water.

In his weary mind, he envisioned long sun flares like fiery fingers reaching down to the earth and stroking the ground and burning him up. It was hard to tell what was real and what wasn't in these lands.

He was becoming weaker and weaker by the moment. He began to stumble and swagger back and forth and fell down. He laid there, face down in the sands. The death bird flew over him, but it didn't attack him because Michael wasn't dead yet. But the spirit in the Spirit Man never dies so the death bird flew away after a while. But the half-dead Michael went into a long dark dream. In his dream, Michael saw the death bird fly back toward him and swoop down upon the cracked earth. The huge death bird began to pick at his flesh and bones and eat him alive. The bird tore off his limbs one by one until he bled to death. Michael saw himself die a slow painful death in his dream only to reappear healed a little bit further away in the same dream. The Spirit Man kicked the huge bird away from his body, watching as it flew away into the black sky.

Michael didn't move in case he was really dead after all. His eyes were closed, and he was at peace, finally, if only for a little bit. But something was tugging at his shirt, yanking him up and shaking him around. He slowly opened his eyes to see the same hands from before, who finally stopped in their assault. One gripped the front of his shirt, and before it moved again, Michael realized the second had been lifted to smack him, trying to get him awake. The hands pointed to a door and Michael nodded, grunted and got up to his feet, finally passing through another door.

This was the second magical blue door that Michael had found and slipped through from one world to another. He disappeared into the deep blue sky of the door and reappeared on the other side of it in a split second, if even that. The door disappeared behind Michael and the floating hands as he stood in the middle of another foreign desert. He was still in the desert but this one had a gentle breeze that felt warm and healing. Up ahead, he saw a toll booth of some kind stuck way out here in the middle of nowhere. It was a rather small booth, adobe tan in color. It had a pitched roof made of red Spanish tile and stood about ten feet tall and six feet wide in all.

Stumbling a little, Michael walked towards the toll booth in the middle of his Dream World. When he got a few feet away from it, he was caught off guard when the door swung open to reveal a beautiful woman missing both hands. The hands that were guiding him flew over to her. Her smile could have rivaled the sun when she beamed and said, "You brought him here? Sweet! Thank you."

The right hand attached itself to her right wrist and she gave the other hand a high five. The left spun in place around her wrist until there was an audible click.

She gave Michael a toothy grin. "Took you long enough to get here, Jackie Jackass. Don't you know it's rude to leave a lady waiting?"

She propped her fists on her hips in a position of mock impatience, though Michael couldn't take his eyes off her hands. They just… attached, as if it was as simple as that. He couldn't even tell where the hands had ended before; they looked as if they'd never been anywhere else than, of course, attached to this woman.

Stunned, Michael fumbled for words which felt stuck deep in his dry throat. "Where am I? I was just in New Mexico."

"New Mexico, New York, New Buffalo, New Hope, New I-Don't-Give-A-Shit. Now you are in West Heaven."

"Heaven?" Michael repeated. "Did I die and go to heaven?"

She laughed. "You didn't die, and this place is hardly heaven. All you have to do is take a good look around you and see this is not heaven but more like hell, don't you reckon?"

"Excuse me, miss, but do you know me?" Michael asked, bewildered.

She shook her head, "Can't say that I remember. Everyone knows you. Or was it that no one does? Choose one, Jackie."

Michael was confused, standing there in silence as rain started to fall, at first a trickle, then suddenly a surging, sudden desert monsoon. A rush of ice cold rain found its way through the back of his loose blue jean shirt and down his bare back, shocking him. He shivered in the rain. Within a few minutes, he was soaked to the bone, shivering in front of the woman with the strange flying hands.

"Well, don't just stand there, stupid," she shouted over the pouring rain and thunder which roared like a lion. "Get your ass in here, Michael! Don't just stand there trying to drown!"

At that moment, Michael leaped through the air like a bouncing deer and landed in the middle of the tight quarters of the booth. He lost his balance and found himself in the arms of this strange woman in the middle of nowhere. He could have sworn that she looked familiar, but he couldn't put his finger on where he had seen her before.

Up close, she was beautiful to behold. Her piercing blue eyes met his for a short spell. She looked a little like Wendy, his ex-girlfriend from New Mexico, but she also looked a little like Magellan Champs from the badlands. She even had bits of Ace of Shook to him. But there was something uniquely her to her features, something he could have sworn he had never seen before. She was beautiful, and his heart began to fill with fondness and maybe even...love?

She pushed him away from her as far as she could in the tight quarters of the tiny toll booth, which was not very far at all. "What the hell are you doing? Is there something on my face? What could possibly be so fascinating that it's keeping you from what needs to be done?!" she yelled.

"You are so—so—" he stuttered.

"What?" she shouted at him. "Look, we don't have time for any of this bullshit. We got to get out of here. You were late, so that will put us dramatically behind schedule. We have to leave before they find us!"

"Who?"

"Hunters, Bat Demons, Strikers, Death Birds! Name it and we got it over here in the DWs! Let's go, Wonder Boy!" the woman yelled.

The rain outside, as if satisfied that it had served its purpose, began to slow, and then finally stopped, the silence much bigger than it had seemed before the pounding rain. The dark skies cleared in the distant horizon and the sun was glowing blood red against the gray skies, sinking slowly toward the horizon. There was still enough light from the fading day that Michael could still clearly see.

The woman in the booth barked some orders. "Follow me! Let's go, Spirit Man!"

Michael darted out of the booth and ran after her. She ran around the corner and dashed about fifty yards or so behind the booth until she came to a halt by the side of a white golf cart which had huge wheels. What was a golf cart doing out here in the middle of nowhere anyways? His new friend jumped into the cart and started the engine.

"Get in, Jackie!" She laughed.

Michael laughed with her. He liked her and her attitude didn't bother him at all. Of course, he was wondering why she brought him here, but it could wait until after their daring escape. He climbed in the small cart and sat next to her on the passenger side. The seat was surprisingly comfortable as she began to drive across the barren lands of the DWs or whatever this place was called.

"Where are we going? Why did you drag me here?" Michael asked her, adjusting his seat belt.

"We are going to Satan's Pass. You better watch your ass in Satan's Pass, or so they say. And as for what we are going to do? Isn't it obvious? We are going to save the world."

"I thought this place was called West Heaven?"

"The gods have a way of fucking with us."

Michael sat, trying to think of what he should ask her next. A million questions flooded his mind, but only one escaped his lips. "What is your name, by the way?"

"What, you don't know that either? What do you know?"

"I know enough. But seriously, what's your name?"

"Dream Tripper, but you can call me Trip for short."

She glanced over at him just as he stifled a yawn. She rolled her eyes and said, "Now try to get some sleep. We got a long trip ahead of us."

Michael nodded. She glanced over at him and then looked straight ahead as they drove across the barren lands for several hours. They followed half-buried train tracks in the sand as much as they could and soon night fell upon the land like a thick blanket of pitch-black darkness. Stars filled up the night like God had spraypainted it with a handful of white dust. God. Heaven. Satan's Pass. All this made Michael feel uneasy as they drove through the sleepless night.

He tried to get some sleep, but sleep would not come as Trip drove to nowhere.

Chapter 3

The night was long and cold as they rode along in their little dune buggy cart.

"Trip, where are we going?" Michael asked.

"Does that matter? We are getting further away from the freaks who are hunting us down."

"It matters. I think I'm here for a reason. I need to find the girl with three eyes."

The buggy slammed to a stop. "There is no girl with three eyes," Trip said.

Michael turned toward her and said, "Then why am I here?"

"Because I dragged your ass here! There is no deeper meaning than that. I figured you of all people could help me."

"Help you with what exactly? Because all I can figure out is that we are stuck in the middle of a wasteland with freaks on our heels." Though in all fairness, he hadn't seen anyone pursuing them yet, not another soul in the world but the two of them. But it seemed imprudent to mention that at this particular moment.

"Look, I'm trying to find two kids. I lost them, and I need to find them. We agreed if we ever got separated that we would meet in Horizon City. Will you help me find them? Please. I need to know that they are okay." Trip spoke without looking at Michael, staring out through the plexiglass windshield of the buggy. Her hands on the wheel tightened, and her jaw seemed to get a little more solid, like she was gritting her teeth. Whatever had happened to those kids, it was clear that Trip blamed herself, and wanted to make it right. Michael had to respect someone who would do whatever it took to do right by kids.

Michael nodded. "Okay." He'd been through plenty of other worlds and situations with little to no explanation before; he didn't need a long, drawn-out reason to help Trip right now. He believed that she was really trying to help people she cared about, and that was enough information to try to help her.

They had been driving through the night, still following the half-buried train tracks in the desert sands. The tracks ran here and there as the sun rose pink, red, and bright orange over the eastern horizon. The land was still flat and barren as they slowed down and came to an old adobe ranch house. The ranch house was surrounded by a long white metal fence and nothing else for miles. There was another wooden sign by the front metal gate that read DW#17. Underneath were words scrawled in white: "Say hell no to heaven -Raven Bones."

"What are we doing here, Trip?" Michael asked.

"Morris Aloof is an old friend of mine. He will help us with provisions and get those stupid ideas of finding the girl with three eyes out of your head."

Trip drove past the sign, turned left and entered through the open gate leading up to the old ranch house.

"Who is Raven Bones?" Michael asked.

"Never mind that," she said. "You wouldn't want to meet him anyway."

So many dreams to dream about. So many visions to see. So many different worlds to visit even though he knew he could not see them all. How many worlds had he been to so far? One hundred? Two? How many places did he forget? And yet he was just as sure that there were no two places alike, and each one, even the ones he had forgotten, had done its part to shape his spirit and his dreams when he left them. He'd learned long ago that it was better not to question the places fate brought him, only to commit to the journey.

Trip and Michael pulled up to the front of the ranch house. She turned off the motor and jumped out of the cart. Michael followed her, reluctant.

A giant-sized man stood on the front wooden porch. Michael guessed that the man had to be at least six-foot-nine and weigh over two hundred and eighty pounds. The man was dressed in blue overalls and wore a blue and gray striped railroad cap on his head. "Satan's Pass" was written across the front of the cap in small red letters. He had long yellow hair and a motorcycle mustache.

"Trip!" Morris Aloof boomed. "I see you brought a special guest with you. Is it Spirit Man?"

"Yes, this is Michael Spirit Man! I wanted you to meet him," she replied, beaming.

But Michael wasn't so sure that he wanted to meet Morris.

Morris Aloof jumped off his porch and hopped down the three steps to the ground. He ran over to Trip and gave her a huge bear hug. He then gave Michael a huge bear hug as well. He let go and stepped back for a moment. Michael forced a smile to his face. Morris must be a good guy if Trip was so friendly with him, right? Maybe he should give the man a chance.

"Glad to meet yah, oh Spirit Man! Heard so much good about you!" Morris said. "Well, hell's bells. Let me show you around these parts of farts."

The giant man walked past them, and they followed him to horse stables nestled in the middle of a huge pecan tree grove. Morris had three healthy and strong horses in his stable that towered over Michael and Trip, who seemed tiny as a doll next to these majestic beasts. Each horse had an unusual fly mask over their heads, each a different color. The fly masks were longer than they needed to be, making the horses' faces look a little like the flies they were being protected from. Each mask had a blue door painted in the middle of their broad snouts.

Morris cleared his throat and looked over at Michael. "Do you like my horses, Spirit Man?" Morris asked. "This here is Applesauce, Beauty, and Patches."

Michael said, "I have a good friend back home that owns horses as well."

"Home? Where is your home?"

"Nowhere and everywhere," said Michael, a bit unsure. He felt like he'd know his home if he set foot there, but he had a hard time figuring out how to describe it to this man, as if the words weren't enough, and so he couldn't find them.

"Never heard of those places," Morris replied.

The blue doors called to him. "Come on, Spirit Man. Come in and never go back."

The strange voices echoed in his mind again and again. Michael's expression turned from friendly to sullen, as he inwardly silenced the echoing calls of the doors.

"I'll show y'all the cornfields tomorrow if that's okay," Morris announced, frowning as if confused at Michael's odd expression. "But for now I bet y'all are hungry as all get out. Let's eat."

Morris looked both sad and worried but there was nothing Michael could do. All he could do was let it go. No use dwelling on the strange, indescribable way he thought of his home; better to focus on what was happening now and make sure he was as prepared for each moment as possible.

"I'm starving," Trip said.

"Me too!" Michael said, deliberately setting his worries aside, at least for the moment.

They followed Morris into his small but quaint ranch house. Michael turned around and looked back at the horses. There was something eerie and burning in their black eyes, the way the horses followed his movement as he left the barn and followed Morris and Trip back toward the dwelling. Crossing the distance between the house and the stable, Michael heard the whispering of the doors again, their plaintive cries asking him to walk through. He looked around but could see no source of the voices, no matter how hard he looked. For a moment, he stood on the porch of the ranch house, listening to the sound of the wind sweeping through the desert and trying to make sense of all that he was feeling.

Nothing. No distant voice of wisdom or temptation, nothing but the sound of the empty desert. Of course. What had he been expecting?

Michael turned around and followed Morris into his house. It looked like Morris lived all by himself in his small home, every piece of it marked by the presence of a single person with a set way of doing things. The ceilings were vaulted and stood about fourteen feet tall altogether. There were three bedrooms, but what were the other two for? Were they guest rooms? But who would want to stay here?

Morris had a delightful kitchen and a fireplace in the far corner of his living room. Morris was having fun boasting and showing off his home, pointing out everyday features like his comfortable furniture with obvious pride. In the corner of the master bedroom, there was a mask laying in clear view on an end table, almost like a favorite book. A striker mask, its white, powdered cheeks bright against the smeared red of the lips. Morris noticed Michael staring and covered it up the very next second, pulling a royal blue cloth over the face like a shroud. "Trophy," Morris muttered under his breath. "Nothing more."

Michael's stomach flopped and grumbled. Morris stopped in the middle of the living room and turned to face Michael. He got closer, face to face. "Let's eat some grub!" he said.

Michael was frozen and stared deep into his host's eyes, half expecting to see burning coals in them like the horses. But he did not see anything except ice-cold blue eyes. Eyes that looked more fake with each passing second. Eyes that looked more dead than alive.

Soon they all sat down together at the small wooden kitchen table. Morris served everyone ham and cheese sandwiches with pickles and chips. Michael dug into the food right away, not bothering to wait for the others.

Morris drank a huge swig from his ruby colored glass and fell into some kind of trance. He looked like he was having some kind of seizure and Michael and Trip stopped eating to observe the event with great concern and worry.

"What's going on, Trip? Is there anything we can do to help him?" asked Michael.

"He's having a seizure. They come and go. It will be all over before you know it. There is nothing we can do for him." Trip barely spared a glance for Morris, continuing to munch on her potato chips as if there was nothing strange about this entire situation.

　　　　　　　　　　　DREAM OF THE SPIRIT MAN

Morris opened his mouth and words poured out, his voice booming as a storm. "I am Raven Bones. Let bleeding clouds rain blood upon the lands! My eyes of fire see now more rails with sharp nails. The sands of time have blown my mind. Try and find the girl with three eyes and we will burn her to her knees for what she has done to the world."

Morris snapped out of his deep trance and stopped trembling. He looked dazed, his eyes closed.

"Are you okay, Morris?" Trip asked at last, looking up from her food to pat Morris's hand gently.

"Oh, fuck a duck. I got to feed the horses. My eyes burn like fire! I got to go," Morris said, jumping to his feet.

"Do you want us to help you?" Trip asked.

Morris spun around, his eyes open and red. "Bad demons are coming."

Morris threw down his napkin on top of the table and bolted out the front door. Trip spilled her drink and it sizzled as it hit the table. Things were beginning to unravel very quickly for them in DW#17.

"We got to get out of here!" Trip yelled, yanking Michael after here.

They ran across the living room and dashed outside. They found Morris standing by his horse corral, swaying on his feet a bit, a blank expression in his eyes as he stared at the three horses lined up by the fence directly in front of him.

"Morris!" Trip screamed but he didn't move, didn't so much as twitch at the sound of her voice.

Morris took the fly masks off his three horses and slipped them into the front pockets of his overalls. The horses' eyes burned like hot coals, flickering red and orange and empty, and this time Trip was there to witness it too. Morris turned to his guests, a mirror of his horses' eyes.

He snarled at them with a wide-open mouth full of white fangs. He snapped his head like he was going to bite them, rearing back. "I am Raven Bones," screamed the mad man. "I am the general. I will blow up your dreams, Spirit Man and Dream Tripper. You will never find the girl with the third eye."

Morris roared with sick laughter and then turned on his heel and ran away. In the blink of an eye Morris Aloof, or rather Raven Bones, was long gone behind the horse corrals and into the far distant horizon to the east.

"Who is Raven Bones?" Michael asked Trip.

"I don't know. Let's just go before he comes back." She shook her head and turned toward where the dune buggy still parked in front of the ranch house. Trip trotted away from the corral, heading toward the cart with an easy loping gait.

"Who is this guy, really, Trip? You don't seem shocked," Michael said as he caught up to her, keeping apace as they began to leave the strange, fiery-eyed horses.

"We don't have time for this right now, Michael. Why do you always have to ask a thousand questions before you take a single action? Let's go now!" Trip yelled.

The ground beneath their feet began to shake and tremble as blue light erupted everywhere, spilling from the ground in sharp spikes like lightning in reverse. The blast was so strong that it blew out all the windows and doors of Aloof's abandoned home. There was a series of explosions that filled up the air all around them. Michael could feel the heat as they both ran toward their little ATV buggy. They jumped into the cart just in the nick of time. Trip put the buggy into gear and hit the gas to the floorboard, whipping the buggy around to shoot away from Morris's home and head out into the vast deserts again. She drove away in a straight line toward the eastern horizon as the world shook and a cloud bloomed behind them.

"Where are we going?" Michael yelled over the rumbling blasts and explosions.

"We are getting the hell out of here!"

Michael couldn't wrap his head around what was happening. If Morris was really on the dark side, then why did Trip bring him to Morris in the first place? Was Trip really a good guy? Too many questions out there and too little answers. Michael looked back once to see Morris's place blowing up, soon engulfed in hungry, towering flames. There were several more explosions as the horses became restless and disturbed by all of the noise and destruction. And in a blinding flash of light, Michael saw a vision of sorts. He saw the devil himself, pitchfork in hand. He smirked and said, "Hey, Jackass. All is well in hell if there is one. But there isn't. So why do you dumb asses believe in such foolishness? It's okay by me. Keeps me in business, chump!"

What a perfect image for a make-believe god. God needed the devil as much as the devil needed God so they could run the show. It was a public relations dream come true.

"You can walk with God or run with the devil," Michael mused. "Either way, we are all fools!"

Chapter 4

They followed the abandoned railroad tracks in the desert sands until they came to the corn fields of DW #19. There were huge stacks of hay on both sides of the tracts, ranging from fifty to seventy-five feet high. They looked a bit like pyramids made of hay in the middle of the vast desert.

"Hey, Trip? I haven't seen you fill up this little golf cart. What does it run on? Love or something?" Michael asked, joking.

"It used to run on diesel in the older days, but all fuel ran out. All of our normal energy sources are gone. Now it runs on my inner thoughts. I tell it to go and it does." She gave him an exaggerated look of smug certainty. "See what happens when things do what I tell them to do quickly? It saves our asses, that's what."

"The power of thought as a fuel...that's cool!" Michael said, choosing to ignore the sarcastic remark.

Trip rolled her eyes at him and graciously moved on, too. "What about your place?" she asked. "Do you still have fuel there?" He liked how she'd said "your place," like the entire world back home was his domicile. Maybe that wasn't a terrible way to think of it.

"We are running out of the fuel source we've been using, pulling it out of the ground," he told her. "Some people are trying to switch to alternatives, but others are greedy and want to suck the world dry."

Trip made a clicking sound with the tip of her tongue and shook her head. "Ain't that just the way," she muttered.

They passed by the long row of haystacks in the DW and acres and acres of dead corn. Flies buzzed in the air all around them. In the distance, dead trees with twisted black limbs choked the horizon. The dead trees looked like black silhouettes of stick figures against the blueish-gray sky.

As they drove along the tracks in the sand, Michael began to wonder. What were they doing here? Did the girl with three eyes even exist?

It was hard to keep his mind out of the dark as they drove down the bleak little trail. This place made him think of the worst of his experiences; the thin, rattling branches of the dead trees reminded him of the arms of the prisoners in Gehenna, the dry, cracked earth like the thirsty ground back in Fort Huachuca. Every row of dead corn seemed to have an arch at the end, but then he'd blink and it would just be a sagging stalk, not an ancient gate. Lots of ghosts in my memories tonight, he thought.

One turn down the track and suddenly they encountered their first obstacle in miles. A giant man stood in the middle of the tracks where they curved in the sand. Both Michael and Trip recognized the old rancher from DW#17. He looked bigger than before, standing tall and mighty.

The cart slammed to a halt, jolting its passengers as Trip slammed on the brakes with a curse. They stopped about twenty-five yards away from the man. It was Morris Aloof all right, wearing one of the crazy fly masks over his face, fire burning in his coal eyes. He wore a long leather coat over his overalls and his ears were a foot long and bat-wing shaped. In some ways, it was almost difficult to tell that this man had ever been Morris Aloof, the one who had so proudly pointed out the beautiful woodcarving on one of his coffee tables in that mild little ranch house.

Two Strikers appeared and walked over to Morris's side and stood next to him. They remained silent as Morris Aloof stepped forward. He rose his arms and said, "I will blow your mind and ignite your bones. The child's eyestone is not all seeing as she would like you to believe. It is as blind as a bat demon. You will never find the girl with the white stone. Nothing you do can change the world. So many little gods have come before you and tried to change the world, but they all failed. Just like you will. Broken bones, broken dreams. Give me a break, Spirit Man. I will break you until you give up. You will never win."

"What the hell is he talking about, Trip?" Michael whispered to Trip.

"Hell if I know," she hissed back. "He's mad in the head. All I know is that it won't end well for us if we don't find a way out of here." She hunched over the wheel of the dune buggy, looking around as if judging a way to get off the track and off road.

"What can I do?" Michael asked, trying to keep his voice low. His heart felt like it was rattling, not beating, in his chest.

"Hang tight!" she muttered. "Things are about to get interesting!"

Michael had no idea how they were going to get out of this mess they were in. Three dozen Strikers came running out of the dead corn fields carrying rifles and machine guns with them. They gathered around Morris and began to hoot and holler, rallying cries of "Kill the Spirit Man!" echoing in the empty air.

A dozen or more scarecrows began growing around them, one after another in the corn fields. Huge wooden death stakes and crosses rammed through the earth and appeared standing there among the rows of corn, swaying in the rising wind, their tattered clothes making their movements seem jerky and strange. Some of the wooden stakes and crosses stood forty feet tall, looming like terrible gods in the broad, empty sky. The scarecrows looked like giants, nailed to wooden stakes and dangling limply from their wrists. The scarecrows looked all the same, dressed in blue overalls, jagged smiles carved into their crooked faces.

Horrible screams and moans came out of the slit mouths. "We will kill you, Spirit Man. Our master, Raven Bones, speaks to us and commands us to kill, to rip the flesh off your bones!" All the scarecrows screamed as one, the effect terrifying as their canvas smiles flapped in the wind. Their voices sounded like branches breaking in a storm, like the distant shrieking of coyotes in the hills.

As the giant demons were ranting in their hellish, hoarse voices, the violences they'd enact and the horrors their victims would endure, Trip tried to focus on her buggy. She rubbed her temples over and over again. She whispered. "Come on, Little Buggy! Think green. Think army. Think tank. Come on, you little fucker, think big!"

Michael had no idea what Trip was talking about or doing to help get them out of this mess, but he trusted her. He must have a reason, beyond her pretty face, that he'd placed all his trust in this foul-mouthed woman. Right?

The cart began to jump up and down and jerk, huge sheets of green metal plates shooting up on the four sides all around them. The green plates covered their heads and for a brief moment, they couldn't see a single thing but the green in front of them. The loud sounds of metal grinding against each other filled up their ears. Michael did not know how Trip was doing this, but she must have a powerful mind's eye to envision something like this. Lights flickered on inside their new tank and a computer monitor swiveled around, showing a 360-degree view all around them.

Trip jumped up and did a little dance. "Yeah, there it is! Trip makes it happen again, whoo hoo! You ain't never seen someone like me, sure as hell!"

Warmth flooded Michael's cheeks as he watched Trip hop around, crowing her victory cry. He cleared his throat and yanked his eyes away from her. "What can I do?" He was beginning to feel like a sack of potatoes being lugged around from one place to another, not contributing enough to the fight.

"All you got to do is use your other sight," Trip said slowly, as if she was saying, "Of course you're the Spirit Man," or something else incredibly obvious.

Pain flared through Michael's head. Other sight? Why did that sound so familiar?

All hell broke loose as the first round of gun fire hit the tank. Bones shouted out, "Fire away! Kill them both!"

Trip popped the tank into first gear, and they began to move forward at a snail's pace, but at least they were moving. The scarecrows took a shaking step closer to them and caught their hands on fire. They threw the fire balls at the tank, but each passed over the tank without harming it. Trip leaned over the control panel and found a red button with an image of an eye in the center. She pressed the big red button and mumbled under her breath, "I wonder what this does?"

A six-foot-long antenna popped out of the top of their tank with a two-foot-wide silver disk at the top. The disk could move in every direction. It revolved around and around, an eye appearing in the center of it. A name popped in Michael's head. The Eye of the Dream Tripper was a weapon, greatly fears by many in the DW. The eye itself had a black pupil with some hints of red and green in the middle of it. A rather thick golden band outlined the eye, making it seem golden in color.

Where had that information come from? It just popped into his head, as if he'd always known it, same as he'd always known his own name. Michael almost looked over his shoulder to see if there was someone who had whispered the knowledge into his ear, dropping it straight into his brain. But of course, there was no one there; this was only how it worked in these strange worlds he visited. Here in the DW, maybe there were some things that everyone knew.

The Eye of the Dream Tripper shot out hundreds upon hundreds of lasers at the Strikers in the fields and along the tracks. The laser killed dozens of Strikers in the matter of a few minutes. The eye shot lasers at the scarecrows in the corn fields, lighting them up from behind for a moment in the light of their explosions. Michael saw the entire mini battle unfold before his eyes on the computer monitor before them. The battle lasted for an hour, the Strikers unable to place a single scratch on the tank. The Eye was both deadly and precise. It killed off hundreds of Strikers during the fight. It blew up and burned down all the scarecrows. Only once the majority of the Strikers had been killed did the Eye stopped spinning, motionless and dream-like, staring fixed into nothingness. But Michael guessed that it would come alive at any given moment if they needed its power and deadly aim.

Trip drove the tank toward Raven Bones who was standing alone in the middle of the tracks. Raven Bones did not move from the spot, just staring them down. Bones was calm as he shouted, "You will never change the world. Even if you find the girl with the white stone, you can never reverse the damage that has been done."

Trip put the tank into cruise control, closed her eyes, and turned away from the controls. The tank ran Raven Bones over, crushing his bones into a pile of dust.

Michael opened the hatch to see what happened to Raven Bones with his own eyes. The corn fields were burned and blackened, huge clouds of smoke drifting over their heads. Bodies from the fallen Strikers lay all around, heads blown off their shoulders so neatly and exactly, Michael almost couldn't believe any machine could be capable of such power. After a few moments, Michael spotted Raven Bones' body sprawled across the half-buried train tracks, pressed down into the dirt, his great limbs broken and akimbo against the buried tracks.

Michael closed the hatch and they drove off in total silence. The tank was still on cruise control and it knew to follow the tracks. After their path ahead was clear, the tank just kept driving, slower than the dune buggy but much more secure. Trip sighed and turned away from the console. "I'm going to try to get some damn shut eye," she told Michael, leaning back in her seat and throwing an arm over her eyes. Within a moment, she seemed to be breathing more deeply. Michael almost couldn't believe it.

For the next few hours, Trip slept while Michael was left wondering if Raven Bones was truly dead or not. After all, how many times did he come back to life? Michael was the last person in this or any other world to think that death was a permanent condition.

It didn't do much good to worry about it now. Maybe Trip had the right idea; maybe there wasn't any good to worrying right now, and he should just rest. He was tired. When was the last time he'd been able to rest, knowing that they were safe? If Trip thought it was safe enough to fall asleep here, then he was going to follow suit. Dead tired, Michael eventually fell asleep, too, as the tank made its way to who knows where.

Chapter 5

Michael slept on, dreaming of the ranch they left. There was a huge explosion at the old ranch house and the three horses jumped into the air. Their hooves crashed down upon the wooden rails of the old horse corral, knocking it down to the ground like so many matchsticks. The horses bolted out of the huge gaping hole there and galloped together, making their way toward their owner's corpse. Their eyes burned with fire and smoke, looking more like dragons than horses as they pounded across the land. The earth shook and trembled under their hooves as the three horses made their way across the barren land. Huge black wings began to sprout out of their backs and with a few powerful strokes of their wings, they glided over the land. Michael saw them as if from the ground, the terrible sweep of their wings as they scorched the sky in their flight. He knew in his heart, beyond a shadow of a doubt, that these creatures meant death to any living soul unlucky enough to fall under their fiery gaze.

The hellscape melted, dissolving into white and gray, and the dream changed to one of the little girl with the white stone. The girl was not clear, her ghost-like spirit standing alone in front of a gigantic black wall. With the surety of a dreamer's logic, Michael knew that the wall separated the dream worlds from the real world. Beyond the little god was a huge kaleidoscope eye painted on the black wall in bright colors. The girl wore a dress covered with tiny rectangular mirrors. She had long black hair and dark brown eyes that spoke of mischief and truth. Her eyes sparked like diamonds. There was a blinding flash of bright blue light and the girl was gone, leaving behind only the vivid, multicolored eye staring straight out at Michael, as if into his very soul.

Michael woke up.

Dragons. Horses. Little gods that looked like little girls.

How old was the girl? Ten? Twelve?

He didn't know. But there was one thing that he was certain of. She was real. No dream he'd ever seen had seemed so real to him; no vision of the potential future had held the sorts of details he'd noticed about the little girl. That thought comforted him as he dozed for a bit longer, the tank still rattling along down the trail.

It was midafternoon before the tank finally came rolling to a stop. The hatch above Michael and Trip opened up and they could feel fresh air. The warm air felt good as they leapt onto their feet and looked out of the hatch for the first time in hours. The deadly eye was sleeping and perfectly still inside the silver disk on top of the tank. The land around them was flat and barren, scorched to the bone.

The tank had stopped only yards away from a steep cliff. A huge suspended bridge spanned the river. They climbed out of the tank and jumped to the ground. There was a wooden sign in front of them that read: DW #21 Bridge over Known Worries. Trip didn't seem to be bothered by any of this. She took out a can of spray paint and put her name on the tank in big, running silver letters. *TRIP'S TANK! HANDS OFF* the letters shrieked in jagged strokes. Then, with perfect precision, Trip leaned in closer and spray painted a skull and crossbones beside her warning, perfectly formed with no running paint at all.

"Do you like it, Michael?" Trip grinned, tossing her spray paint back into her bag.

"Sure, but what are we going to do now? Will the tank go over the bridge?" he asked, pointing at the bridge. "Do we have to leave it here? What's next?"

"I don't know," Trip snapped back. "I don't have any answers right now for your questions. But I found some food in one of the compartments in the tank. Let's eat."

"Do we really have time for that? We don't know how much of a lead we have. We can eat inside the tank while it moves, if it can make it over the bridge."

She turned to him and shrugged, "Michael, there is only a handful of times we can have a picnic looking at such a view. Let's just relax for now and worry about that later."

Michael gave her an incredulous look. "Look who's all relaxed all of a sudden. Aren't you feeling any urgency?"

Trip sighed and shook her head, looking back down the trail, toward the direction they'd come from. "Look. Back there, I knew that Raven Bones had to die, but..." She pressed her lips together in a thin line, still looking off down the road. "I need a break, I guess. I don't feel guilty about running him down like the son of a bitch he was, but I keep thinking about how at the last moment, I wanted to turn the wheel away." She turned back to Michael, tilting her chin up defiantly. "So. Let's take a break. Sound good?" She put her fists on her hips as if she wanted him to pick a fight with her.

What could an extra little bit of waiting hurt? "Okay," Michael said.

Trip didn't seem to get shaken that much, so if she needed a break, then they could afford it.

He gave her a big smile as they sat down together on the ground in front of the tank. They devoured the food, packed sandwiches and wrapped cookies that Trip had found in the tank's storage, but the taste was flavorless to Michael. Maybe that was a side effect because it was food that was dreamed up? Or maybe he had too many hovering, unanswered questions to enjoy the food in front of him....

"Who is the girl with the white stone, Trip?" Michael asked quietly, munching on the last few bites of a flavorless BLT. He couldn't get that image from the dream he'd had earlier out of his mind, the little girl turning to him with that smile on her face, her eyes sparking with light from within.

"She is a legend in this land. To be honest, I'm not sure if she is real or not," Trip said, taking a big bite of some kind of cookie with rainbow sprinkles. Maybe the food only tasted bland to Michael; Trip didn't seem to mind it at all, polishing off three sandwiches and two cookies before Michael could get through his first sandwich. "From my experience, I'd chalk her up as more imagined than real, personally," Trip continued.

　　　　DREAM OF THE SPIRIT MAN

"I had a dream about her last night," Michael said, looking at his food. It didn't look any different from any other piece of food he'd ever eaten before, so why couldn't he taste it? "She seemed like something real to me then. And I've learned that some dreams are worth listening to if they seem real enough."

"Well, sometimes dreams have meaning and sometimes they don't," Trip said around a mouthful of cookie. "The girl with the three eyes is a myth of the DW, Michael, nothing more. Stop chasing fairy tales. That won't help anybody."

Michael opened his mouth only to shut it again. She had a point. It was only a dream, in the end. Just because the girl felt real didn't mean she was not real.

They heard some loud rumbling noises in the far distance. They both got to their feet and looked back the way they'd come, listening closely. The river nearby sounded incredibly loud, now that they were trying to be completely silent.

"Trip?" Michael murmured. "What's that sound?"

She shook her head grimly. "Whatever it is, they are coming. We better get going."

Michael nodded. It didn't really matter who or what was coming. Besides, he had a pretty good idea what it was. The dragon horses were going to find a way to bring their master back to life. There was birth and death and birth again. Michael knew that if he could come back to life again and again, Raven Bones could too. That part of his dream, apparently, wouldn't leave him the time to question it before making sure it came true.

Michael and Trip climbed back into the tank and the hatch closed over their heads once again. She pressed a green button and the tank began to roll forward towards the bridge. The bridge was paved, one of the first paved areas he had seen in this world. It was filled with potholes, but it was still a road. Michael took a deep breath as the tank rolled onto the suspended bridge over the rushing waterfall below them. When they got to the middle, the tank shut down and stopped. It made a disturbing high-pitched whining sound and then quit moving altogether.

After a moment, the console before them sputtered, leaving Trip and Michael in total darkness. "Damn it," Trip muttered.

The hatch opened above their heads and Trip jumped toward the ladder, pulling Michael to climb up with her and look out at the outside world. The day was perfect. Plenty of sunshine and clear blue sky above them with not a single enemy in sight. So what had made the tank stop?

"I'll check it out," Trip said, hopping out through the hatch and climbing down from the tank. Michael followed her in climbing out, standing on the ground as Trip circled the tank, checking its sides.

The silver disk on the top of the tank was not awakened as of yet, so there probably weren't enemies upon them just yet. At least there was that, Michael thought with relief.

"What's wrong with the tank?" Michael asked.

"She quit on us, I guess. Maybe it's got a thorn stuck in its paw," Trip snapped sarcastically. "I don't know everything, Michael! Why don't you fix it with all your questions?"

"I can try, but I don't own a tank at home."

Michael tried climbing back into the dark and pushing buttons on the console, kicking at the giant treads, yanking at any area of the plating that seemed to be sticking out, but nothing started the tank back up. It sat there in the middle of the suspended bridge like a dead, green toad.

The rumbling sound was a lot closer than before. Trip looked up and over at the growing cloud of dust. An explosion in the distance made them stumble back.

"The horses are coming to wake up their master of disaster," Michael said. Again, that sense of surety, that this was information he knew for certain, though he had no memory of where he'd learned it. Trip shot him a worried look, but only shook her head at last and turned back to face the growing cloud in the distance.

"Something really wanted our asses to be stuck right here, so I guess we'll be here," she muttered. Michael could only nod. Trip was right. It was like a supernatural force had stopped the tank here, putting Trip and Michael in their places for the show. Only violence could possibly be coming for them.

There was too much blood staining the earth, too many questions. What was it all for? Too bad there were very few answers. Was this all a game or entertainment for some kind of deranged deity? Was there any point at all?

Chapter 6

The wind blew across the wastelands, tearing up the few plants that clung to the surface. Little rocks, blown by the gusts, skittered over the suspension bridge as if they, too, were trying to run away. Michael turned to Trip. "Is there any way we can see what's going on?" he said, raising his voice to be heard over the loud wind.

She put her hands on her hips. "Oh, yeah, sure, of course. Let me just grab my magical binoculars that let us see around the curvature of the earth. Why didn't I think of that? Come on, Michael, what do you think?"

"I was just asking," Michael said defensively. "Geez."

"You ask me every time something happens!" Trip snapped, throwing her hands in the air. "I have all the same information right now that you do, Spirit Man, believe it or not, and I can't see anything about what's coming this way with my bare eyes."

"Maybe the deadly eye has something we could use to see a far distance?" Michael suggested.

"I thought you had super vision or something. Just use that," Trip said, rolling her eyes.

Michael had gone on so many adventures, it was hard to remember all of the powers and abilities he'd picked up along the way. Not all of them were consistent from journey to journey, either. He'd learned to stop keeping track and just let them come back when he needed them, like they always did.

Trip sighed and said, "Just focus as much as you can and then you should be able to see what you want." She said it so authoritatively that Michael instinctively knew she was right; no wonder he was the one asking questions all the time!

All right, then, time to focus like Trip directed and see what came of it. He closed his eyes and took a deep breath, trying to clear his mind as completely as he could so he could focus on improving his vision. He exhaled one long breath, feeling the emptiness of his lungs before he opened his eyes again.

Michael focused as hard as he could, squinting, trying to force his eyes to peer into the distance, far beyond his usual range of sight. At first, there was nothing, just dust and gray blurriness in the direction of the noise. Then, suddenly, it was like a switch flipped in his brain and everything grew sharp and clear. Three horses with wings were flying toward the area still filled with black smoke, their wings stretched huge and dark against the blue sky.

"What do you see?" Trip asked. Her voice sounded the same as it ever did, but it was strange to hear it without looking at her, hearing her voice over the grim image of the terrible flying beasts before his eyes. Michael didn't answer her, focusing on following the horses in his vision. They suddenly folded their wings in and dove down toward the ground; Michael's vision tracked them in their descent, following all the way back to the ground, though some part of his brain said his line of sight should be interrupted. But he didn't dare question it, instead watching the beasts come to a thunderous landing, then slow to a trot down the track. The three horses stopped a few yards away from where Raven Bones' corpse lay, the imprints of Trip's tank still marking his body with how he'd died. The horses shrieked, a high-pitched noise full of sorrow and hate. How could Michael hear that, too? Was his hearing enhanced as his sight in this moment, or was he merely hearing phantom sounds? Impossible to tell for sure.

A huge cloud of black smoke drifted over this incredible scene. Blue and white lights streaked through the dark angry smoke-filled sky as one lightning bolt after another hit the ground all around the horse's hooves. Each time a lightning bolt hit the earth below, it lit up the entire area, and Michael watched with horror as the bodies of the Strikers began to twitch, jerk, and leap up to their feet. With each strike of the lightning, another Striker woke up, jolting alive. The Strikers rose their hands up into the air and they all screamed into the howling wind.

Lightning stuck Raven Bones' body six times in rapid succession. These bolts were so powerful that they hit the ground through Raven Bones' chest, scorching through, and the thunder rumbled the earth below. Raven Bones' chest cavity stretched, as if something was pushing out from the inside, and then the breastbone broke in half, splitting the dead man's chest open like a book. Out of the ruined carcass of Raven Bones' chest, a figure wearing a black hood and a fly mask rose. He looked up to the howling clouds, his eyes glowing red.

Bones threw back his hood and screamed out, "Let's go hunting for the Spirit Man and Dream Tripper!" His voice rang out clear as if Michael was standing a mere ten feet away, the hatred hot in the dead man's voice. For a moment, Michael thought he saw behind the mask, a familiar face, not the face of Morris, but someone else.... Someone else he knew who had also come back from the dead to follow Michael around.

The Strikers roared in thunderous applause for Raven Bones' revival. Shaking their weapons and their fists, the small army began to move in a great crowd, pushing and shouting. A huge cloud of dust rose into the air as they ran forward, obscuring Michael's view of the scene.

Michael blinked, his eyes watering as if the dust from the road had been blown into his eyes. He shook his head, blinking away the tears until the dust cleared, leaving him adjusting back to normal vision. "They are alive and coming for us," he gasped, looking to Trip.

"Who?" she asked, looking between Michael and the dust cloud rising down the tracks.

"Them! The Strikers, Raven Bones, the monster horses, all of them!"

The Deadly Eye creaked on top of the tank, then slowly started spinning, its speed growing faster and faster as Trip grinned. "Bring it on!" she cried with a war-like whoop.

Michael could feel it in his belly. Hellfire was coming, heading right for them, but he wasn't afraid because the Deadly Eye was on their side. It was a good thing, at least, that it had not gone down with the rest of the tank.

Raven Bones' men were within range of normal sight, rushing forward. The Deadly Eye kept spinning but didn't shoot any of its lasers as the army of Strikers drew closer and closer. The ground seemed to shake, and Michael's nerve began to falter, just a little bit.

"Uh, any chance you think we should run?" Michael said to Trip. "We might be able to make it, we've still got a pretty good lead."

"The tank gave up," Trip answered, shaking her head and turning to spit onto the bridge. "Without it and the Eye, we'd be run down in a matter of hours at most. At least with this we will have the Eye and we can hide inside the tank until the battle is over. Unless you care to remember other powers that you got?"

Raven Bones cried out, "Kill them all! Bring their heads to me and destroy their souls!" His voice boomed and echoed like the clap of thunder in the empty air between his army and the bridge.

A large group of death birds and flying Bat Demons appeared in the sky. Some of their wing spans were almost twenty-five feet across as they flew overhead. Hundreds of these black flying monsters sped across the sky, heading toward Michael and Trip.

"Crap!" Trip yelled. "Get into the tank, and fast!"

They took off running, heading for the tank, and barely managed to close the hatch before a death bird swooped down, its deadly talons making terrible metal-screaming sounds as they scraped against the tank's exterior panels. The silver disk on top of the tank began to spin around and around, shooting off lasers at the birds and bat demons that swooped too close. The lasers were both deadly and precise as they hit the bats and birds, exploding them into uneven, bloody bits and pieces. Within ten minutes, hundreds of bats and birds were shot down, their bodies littering the bridge. Michael and Trip huddled inside the dark tank, listening to the sound of the great feathery, leathery bodies thudding to the ground around them outside.

Another small group of death birds flew in the sky, each carrying a silver pouch in its claws. These birds cried out as they dropped the small pouches. Upon impact with the ground, a huge explosion shook the bridge. Michael and Trip held onto each other as they tumbled in the tank, landing sharply on their sides. Huge chunks of the bridge crumbled and fell to the river below. Only the mid-section of the bridge remained intact when Michael got up to his feet and climbed up to cautiously open the hatch and survey the damage around them. The Deadly Eye finished off the last few death birds and bat demons with fatal precision.

The army of Strikers, with Raven Bones as their general, reached where the bridge had once begun, before the death birds dropped those terrible satchels. Now, where the bridge used to be was just a pile of rubble littered with the bodies of death birds and demons. How ironic: their own birds made it so that the army couldn't reach Michael and Trip, and the Strikers couldn't attack the tank. Without the birds, they had no ranged attacks, and the bridge was unpassable from either side now. The Deadly Eye spun rapidly, ensuring that any other bird would be similarly dispatched of.

"Can we call this a victory?" Michael asked Trip.

Trip pounded her hands on the control board. "How is this a victory? We are stranded in the middle of a river with no way out but down to our deaths."

"There is always a way, Trip, and we will find a way."

Chapter 7

Michael and Trip got out of the tank and jumped onto the pavement. The one part of the bridge that was still standing felt like it was swaying to the right and left, making both of them freeze where they stood, but it settled uneasily after a few moments. For the time being, at least. Most of the bridge was blown to smithereens and gone. Huge chunks of the bridge had fallen into the river, making the water splash and froth around the giant blocks of the structure. They were cut off on either side, and frankly the part that remained didn't seem to have much longer left in its stability.

"What do we do now, Trip?" Michael asked, putting one hand on the tank for balance. He didn't want to trip over a piece of rubble and fall over; somehow, he got the sense that if anything fell too far off balance here, the bridge wouldn't survive it.

"Why do I always have to be the one to get us out of these messes?" Trip shot back, standing frozen on the bridge, apparently sensing the instability of the bridge, as well.

"Well, isn't this place your home?"

"I don't have a home, Michael. Or if I did, I forgot about it long ago. I'm just as lost as you are in this dream world." Trip slowly moved closer to the tank, putting a hand on it to steady herself, too. "Shows how little you know about me, I guess."

He fell silent for a while, not looking right at her. "I'm sorry. I didn't know that. I thought you lived here, you know it so well."

She glanced at him, then shrugged. "I just know it because I've been here a while. That doesn't mean it's my home or that I know what to do every moment. So stop putting that pressure on me. It's not fair to defer to me when you're in this as much as I am. Hell, probably more."

Michael sighed and nodded. "You're right. But what are we going to do? We are on top of a bridge with nowhere to go that might fall apart at any second."

Trip shook her head, the anger gone from her voice. "Fuck," she whispered, "I don't know. I just don't know."

She turned to the sky and Michael followed her gaze. There was a black dot in the distance getting closer and closer. He squinted, trying to make out what it was.

"What is it, Michael?" Trip asked. "Can you tell?"

"I don't know. We've seen all sorts of stuff out here. It could be a bat demon, a death bird, or something else entirely. Do you think we should get back inside the tank?"

"No!" A strange voice not belonging to Trip boomed through the air. Was it answering Michael's question?

The creature in the air got closer and closer, descending rapidly through the air. It dropped so close that Michael saw that it was not an evil creature at all, but a young man in cargo pants and a light blue shirt with large white bird wings, gliding down to where they were. He flew as easily as some people breathed, rocking on his broad wings through the air in his descent. The man landed gently on the bridge, causing it to sway back and forth, but he just smiled as the stone rocked. Michael and Trip both reached out to steady themselves on the tank again, watching the man warily. In the land of the dream, it was wise to treat every stranger politely, but cautiously, until they showed their true colors, in Michael's experience.

"Hello, boys and girls of the DWs!" the young man said cheerfully. "My name is Atlas! Good to see you, Spiritman, and the great lady, Dream Tripper. I see you are in quite a pickle."

The man was covered with several colorful tattoos, swirling designs full of bright colors. But the most distinct tattoo the young man had was a snake tattooed along his right arm, its fangs long and ruby red. He saw Michael looking at it and grinned, flexing his arm, making the snake's scales ripple. It looked almost alive.

"How did you get here?" Michael asked the man slowly. "And how did you find us?"

"I came from the north country and saw the commotion down

below." Atlas gave a shrug, which made his wings rise and fall over his shoulders, too. "I figured I would lend a hand, but the fighting seemed already done. You ever catch a falling leaf? It's like trying to catch a dream. You reach higher and higher, but you never touch any of your dreams." He grinned and rocked back on his heels, a dreamy smile on his face.

"Right, dreams and height, but let's focus on the situation at hand. Can you get us off this bridge before it collapses under us, Atlas?" Trip asked.

Atlas cocked his head to one side, looking at her with a friendly smile. "By the sound of it, I would say that this bridge is going to fall and crash to the river below any minute now."

"Yeah, hence my fucking urgency," Trip snapped.

"Can you help us or not?" Michael asked. It was all well and good for the man with the wings to lollygag. If this bridge fell, Atlas would be the one hovering in the air waving goodbye as Michael and Trip were lost to the raging waters below.

"I will tell you a story first," Atlas said. "And then I will throw you a ten-pound fishing line. That should help keep you from drowning."

"We don't have time for any stories," Michael growled. "The bridge is going to fall apart, and we are going with it."

Trip shook her head, her voice wobbling just a bit. "I don't want to die. Not again."

Atlas shook his head with a cluck of his tongue and a grin. "Nobody is going to die today. So, let me tell you my story. A story of hope is always a good thing to have with you in these dark times. The girl with three eyes is such a story. Michael, you need to find her and bring her back to your world. She is the only one who can save it."

"Why? How can one little girl save the world?" Michael asked.

The bridge creaked and he leaned hard against the tank. Trip swore under her breath.

"I don't know how the story ends, just the steps you need to get there. Follow the sun and push on. Never give up."

Trip rolled her eyes. "Can you help us now? Or do we have to be even closer to our doom before you'll shut up and save us?"

"Sure!" Atlas said with a smile. "Now that the important stuff is done, I can help you out of this situation, I suppose."

The young man dug deep into his pocket and pulled out a spool of ten-pound fishing line. He grabbed the fishing line and tied it around the base of the Eye in a double hangman's knot and tugged on it two times to make sure it was tight. The bridge groaned and tilted several feet to the far left. Huge chunks of concrete fell off the bridge and crashed down into the river below them and Trip gave a shriek, her fingers scrabbling at the side of the tank as if to get a grip in its thick metal siding.

Atlas tugged on the line once more for good measure and said, "Hurry up now and hold on to the tank tightly."

"How in the hell is this going to work?" Trip asked.

Michael shrugged and scrambled on top of the tank, holding on tightly to the fishing line above the spinning eye. He took a good look all around him. Huge chunks of the bridge were missing. The bridge swayed and Trip lost her balance crashing into the side of the tank. Michael reached down for her and she grabbed his hand, climbing on top of the tank with him. Michael accidentally pulled a bit too hard and Trip lost her footing, falling into his arms. The wind howled as the bridge began to crumble in every direction. Trip closed her eyes and leaned in, holding onto Michael tight as the bridge jerked violently from side to side. Her fingers gripped his shirt so tightly her knuckles went white.

"I'm sorry," Trip said, her face buried in Michael's shirt. He almost couldn't make out what she was saying against the crashing sound of rocks falling into the river, loud splashing all around them.

Michael blinked and squeezed her tightly, his other arm looped around the fishing line tied to the Eye. "What for?"

"For dragging you here. For pulling you into this mess again. I don't want to be alone again." There was a note of near hysteria in her voice, like she thought she had to spit all this out before they tumbled below.

Michael looked down at her and kissed her forehead. "It's okay, Trip. If there was a way I had to go, well, I'm glad it was with you."

"I lo—"

There was a jolt and Atlas sprang into the sky, catching a gust of wind. The metal beneath them groaned and the eye of the tank snapped off, yanking Trip and Michael into the air. Trip yelped and Michael grabbed on firmly to the Eye and the line, clinging for dear life. They closed their eyes, waiting for the hard crash into the river below. After a moment, Michael blinked open his eyes to see not water, but the bright yellow cliffs of the steep canyon getting closer and closer. It was like they were floating. The sensation felt funny and, for a moment, Michael thought he had died. He closed his eyes but still saw the clear blue sky.

They were gliding in midair as they passed by the remaining part of the bridge that was standing on the other side of the river. The paved road across the bridge was completely gone.

Michael paused, admiring the scenery, noticing that Trip was shaking, her face buried in his chest, her fingers still knotted tightly in his shirt.

"Don't worry," Michael whispered. "We are going to be alright."

High above them, he could see the fishing line glinting like a silver thread in the sky, and Atlas flying with great ease and purpose, holding the line like it and the people tied to it weighed nothing. Far below, the land seemed like a patchwork of textures, greens and browns with the occasional strip of blue river. Even though they had to be thousands of feet in the air, Michael found himself feeling peaceful. There was so much to do when they landed, but for now, it was just him, and Trip in his arms, flying like a kite behind Atlas above, no enemies to bother them. For a moment, it felt like this was nothing more than a good dream.

Fifteen minutes later, Atlas successfully glided them over to the other side of the river, their feet brushing against the dirt before landing on solid ground. It was a perfect landing, as smooth as silk. A rush of fresh air hit them. They looked up at the sky as Atlas flew down to the ground. The young man started winding up the thread as Trip took one more shuddering breath and broke apart from Michael, gazing up into his eyes. Michael broke away, unsure he was worthy to see the vulnerability in her eyes and said, "You did it. Thank you, Atlas. You saved us." He wanted to glance back at Trip, try to get a sense of what she was feeling, but he had a feeling she'd prefer the privacy to get her wits about her before trying.

Atlas laughed, untying the string from the top of the eye. "It was nothing. You've saved my life plenty of times, Spirit Man. It was the least I could do." He waggled his eyebrows. "Don't say you don't remember, or it'll break my poor little featherweight heart."

His face went a shade paler and he stopped winding the string into a bundle, kneeling over. His left wing twitched, stretched sharply out into the air behind him, and then drooped like its muscles had suddenly been cut. Trip ran over to him and said, "Are you alright?"

Atlas winced and stretched his arms; the left wing fluttered but stayed down, while the right stretched just like his arms.

"Oh, I'm fine, don't you worry," Atlas said with a tired grin. "Great flying weather. Haven't pulled that much around for years. Reckon I better sit here and rest for a bit." He yawned and shook himself. His right wing gave a shiver that made his feathers rustle, and his left valiantly wobbled, though not as strongly.

Trip reached out her arms as if to give Atlas a big hug but seemed to think better of it and put her hand on his shoulder. She stood on her toes and gently placed a kiss on Atlas' cheek with a gentle smile. "Thank you. Really and truly, thank you."

Atlas smiled, turned red and ducked his head bashfully. "You are welcome. But I'm not the hero here. You two are the real heroes, going to find the girl with three eyes. You two are going to save the world together." He touched the tips of his fingers to his cheek. "Thanks for the kiss, though. Quite nice of you."

Trip laughed and rolled her eyes. "Yeah, well, you still saved our bacon out on that bridge. I'd say that's worth a peck on the cheek."

Near where the bridge used to begin over the river, there was a young tree, and Atlas settled beneath it, leaning his back against the bark. He finished winding up the fishing line and closed his fingers around it and held it for quite some time, staring at the bundle of string in his hands. Michael thought for a moment that the winged young man had fallen asleep, but then Atlas looked up at the sky and with a soft smile said, "Do you have time for one more story of mine?"

This time, Trip didn't protest. "Yeah, a story sounds nice," she said, sitting down on the ground in front of him. She looked up at Michael, and he saw no trace of the vulnerability that had been so deep in her eyes when they landed. But she did smile at him and pat the ground next to her. He sat and smiled back, giving her a little space on the ground.

"All right," Michael said, looking to Atlas. "Tell us a story, man of the winged world."

"Ha! Happily," Atlas grinned. "All right, you kids and kiddos, here is my story. There is no god or devil here in this DW. But there are many evil spirits hellbent on destruction and demise that will make damn sure that you don't find the girl with three eyes. These dark spirits know only of one craft and that is the cursed art of murder. In other words, they don't want you to save the worlds. This is your battle. The DW is full of magic and surprises and good, but there are many who would prefer to see it destroyed. You must be brave. Don't give up. Find the girl with the three eyes before it is too late." He leaned his blonde head back against the tree's bark, looking up through the leaves to the blue sky beyond with a look of wistful reverence on his face.

There was a long moment of silence between them as Atlas continued to stare up into the sky. Then he seemed to come awake again, blinking and looking back to Michael and Trip like he was remembering they existed. "Like I told you before, there are no gods or devils here. But Raven Bones is one of the evilest spirits that roam these parts. He'll give you hell and then some on your journey, but still, you must push on, my dear friends. You must get to Satan's pass."

Michael nodded and said, "How do we get there?"

"Follow the long winding road to Mendoza Mountain. After that, you will be on your own. I don't know what your journey looks like after that, and maybe no one knows. Perhaps you will meet someone there that can tell you the next steps to take. But be warned, no one that I know has ever made it past Satan's Pass."

Atlas stood up and stretched up tall on the tips of his toes, his wings stretching out. He must have a wingspan of fifteen feet or better, Michael mused in awe. Both wings stretched now with the full glory of Atlas' strength. "You better get going now," Atlas said. "It will take a while to walk, and while the bridge will deter Bones for a while, they will catch up to you again. That's the way the story has to go."

Trip stood and went to Atlas, reaching out to give him a tight hug. "I'll miss you." She pulled back and grinned up at him, giving him a light punch on the shoulder. "And I hope you know I don't say that lightly, especially to people who rip up my poor tank."

"I appreciate the honor it is, indeed. Thank you, dear!" Atlas chuckled. "You are too kind. Ah, a moment before you go. I almost forgot that you guys are going to need this!"

Atlas tossed the spool of fishing line to Michael, who caught it in midair. Atlas also pulled out two small cap guns from deep within his cargo pants and handed them over. "You never know when this stuff might come in handy. Use it well to defend our cause."

"What is our cause?" Michael asked, pondering the tiny red cap gun in his hand.

"To save the world, baby!" Atlas replied. "And to make it out of here alive!"

Michael put the gun in his pocket and looked over at the young man. "Before you go, I have a question for you, if that's all right?"

"Shoot." Atlas rocked back on his heels, his wings waving gently behind him to help him keep his balance.

"How old are you?" Michael asked.

The feathers on Atlas' wings ruffled and puffed up as his chest swelled. "I am over seven hundred thousand years old. I was born before there were even eyes in the universe." He winked at Michael. "I blinked first."

"Thank you for answering my question," Michael said, somehow sure that the man was telling the truth.

The wind caught Atlas' wings as if on command, pulling the winged man up a good twenty-five feet into the air in a moment's breath. Atlas waved down at Michael and Trip as he was lifted like a paraglider into the air. Michael and Trip waved back, their arms like pinwheels.

Atlas grinned and yanked out his left eye. The instant he did, another eye rolled in to take its place from somewhere deep in his skull, this one's iris a different color than the first. Atlas grinned and yelled, "You never know what will be helpful come high tide. Take this with you! Good luck!"

The eyeball fell toward Trip, who yanked off her hand and threw it at the eyeball that was about to fall over the edge of the cavern. Her hand caught the eyeball in the nick of time and flew back up to Trip, who took it in her attached hand with a look of disgust written on her face.

"What in the hell does he think I'm supposed to do with this eyeball, Michael?" Trip asked as her hand screwed back on. As she held the eyeball in her hand, she soon noticed something unusual and different about the eye. It was like it was made of plastic or fiberglass, hard and gleaming in the palm of her hand.

"I don't know. Can you look through it?" Michael asked, looking at the eye as she held it in her outstretched palm.

"Can I look through it? Really, Michael? It's not even real. It's made of plastic, jackass."

Michael just smiled and shrugged. He couldn't explain it, but he often was very intuitive about the things around him, sensing what was to be done next even when there was no logical or rational reason he should know.

Trip glared at him and said, "Michael, I don't want this freaking creepy ass eyeball. You take it! I'm already excited to wash my hands and get any trace of this thing off me."

"Nope!" he said, holding his hands palms up to her. "You caught it. It's all yours now!"

"Fuck you," she snapped at him, but he ignored her ire. Something in his gut said that the eyeball was supposed to stay with her, at least for now, and if she was annoyed about it, then she'd just need to deal with it until it wasn't supposed to be hers anymore.

"Come on, Trip. We gotta get out of here. No time to focus on who's got to keep a hold on Atlas' eye."

He put the spool in his right breast pocket and started walking, his hands behind his head. Trip was about to throw the eyeball at Michael or try to look through it, but she slipped it into the pocket of her pants instead, then jogged to Michael's side.

"You wanted me to take charge more often?" Michael asked, "Well this is me taking charge. Let's go!"

Trip glared at him and huffed through her nose. As if looking for something else to aim her anger at, she turned to the eye where it had lain on the ground after Atlas dropped them off. It looked almost pitiful, just the long pole leaning in the grass with the eye at the top. "What are we supposed to do with this, by the way? My tank is gone, and we can't just leave the eye here! What will we do when Bones and his lackeys attack us again?"

Michael wasn't sure about the last question, but he had a gut feeling about how they could bring the eye with them. He went up to the eye, crouched down, and said, "Thank you for all the work you've done, but I need to ask you to do something else for us. This size isn't really helpful right now. Do you mind changing shape for us so we can get out of here?"

The eye swiveled toward him, looked him up and down, and blinked slowly as if nodding, then began to spin its iris around and around. The eye spun faster and faster, folding in on itself until it was about the size of a credit card. Michael grinned at Trip and said, "Sometimes you just have to ask nicely."

She scoffed and folded her arms. "Yeah, well, if I'd known it was that easy, I'd chat politely to more of my problems, too."

Michael put the eye into his pocket and started following the path along to their destination. Trip paused for a few seconds, then ran to catch up with him, slipping her arm through his as they walked on and on to nowhere.

The girl with three eyes stood alone on top of a small hill. She was

       DREAM OF THE SPIRIT MAN

dressed in a long sleeve white blouse covered in hundreds of tiny mirrors that bounced light over all the worlds. She looked down at the river, watching Michael and Trip run one direction while on the other side, the army debated the best way to go forward.

"Why are they so slow? It's not a fun chase if one of the groups aren't actually chasing." The girl with three eyes pondered the events below. They could be so boring, the ones below, if she wasn't there to give them a nudge in the fun direction.

She hummed and tapped her foot against the ground before a grin grew large on her features. She slammed her foot on the ground and the river's water shrank down in one place, shallow enough to let a modest army cross it without much strife.

She waited a bit more, but the army still piddled by the bridge, wasting their time and hers. She grew frustrated that the army still hadn't found the way across she had so generously made for them. Didn't they appreciate all the work she was doing to get this show on the road?

She wrinkled her nose and shook her head. "If you want something done, you have to do it yourself."

She shimmied and twirled around twice. When she was done, she looked like a bat demon. She jumped down and flew to the army, approaching Bones with confidence. "Sir, we found a way across the river. It's about two miles downriver, but it's shallow enough for us to pass."

Bones glanced at her, but she radiated sincerity in the form of one of his many underlings. Besides, it wasn't as if Bones was the sort of general who knew each and every one of his men; he was the sort of leader who believed that his followers were disposable and interchangeable and acted accordingly.

Bones nodded, trusting the word of the random bat demon, and drew his breath to order the troops. "Follow the river and find the shallow place to cross!" he boomed.

The demons and warriors began to make their disorderly way in the direction Bones had ordered, and the girl with three eyes easily lost herself in the crowd, letting them flow around her like water as she slipped away. Once she was clear of the army, she smiled to herself and took to the skies, landing back on her hill to resume her watch over what was happening.

The army was crossing the river just fine and Michael and Trip's lead was growing shorter and shorter. Bones and his army would gain ground quickly, especially since Michael and Trip didn't have their tank anymore.

"Wait, is it wrong to let the bad guys have an advantage without helping Trip and Michael?"

The girl with three eyes pondered aloud, tapping her finger against her chin. Maybe she should level the playing field again…so to speak.

She grinned and squashed her hands together. The land rose up and squashed half the army like the slap of a god's palm on a bunch of bugs. The demons screamed out and cried for help, but she just laughed, watching as the earth dragged them screaming underneath it. The rest scattered, managing to escape the wrath of the suddenly shifting, folding land.

After this, Sarah Eyestone giggled like all the little gods do. She laughed at the demons and their misery that she created for them. How amusing, their scrambling, their desperate attempts at survival. Didn't they know how tiny they were? How easily snuffed? It was hysterical, and she laughed for quite a long time.

In the far distance, Michael could hear a soft child's laugh and wondered what was so funny. Then he shrugged and chuckled too.

Chapter 8

Michael and Trip walked for ten more days before the environment around them changed. There were rather large white sand dunes which rolled like ocean waves to their far left. Beyond these flowing sand dunes were a group of tall majestic mountains in the eastern horizon. In front of them was a huge dark green forested mountain. At the base of the mountain was a rather large dark entrance to a tunnel which went all the way underneath the mountain itself. Michael shuddered at the thought. This was Satan's Pass and they were ready to enter it. According to Atlas, nobody ever came out of the dreadful place alive. Well, Michael would see about that. Death was hardly a deterrent to him.

"What are those white dunes called?" Michael asked, nodding to the left and avoiding the very mention of Satan's Pass.

"Yuma hills," she whispered, a sense of quiet honor in her voice. "They are so pretty, don't you think? They look like rolling ocean waves made out of sand as soft as a cloud."

Michael looked up at the majestic mountain that towered high above them. Tall pines and aspens grew on top of the mountain and a few hawks flew overhead. It was hard to believe that such an idyllic scene could hold the dangers that Atlas had warned them about.

"Better watch your ass in Satan's Pass," Michael mused quietly, chuckling at the rhyme. Trip nodded solemnly beside him.

The trees grew taller, looming over them as they walked further up into the pass, the land getting rockier and emptier except for the giant trees stretching high into the sky. They took a corner around the path and there, hovering in the sky, was a neon sign directly above them that read "Satan's Pass" in flashing neon green. Below those words was a warning in bright neon red: "One way in and no way out!" Underneath that was a rather unflattering caricature of

Michael with his head chopped off and the words, "Die, Spit Man," drawn in shaky letters with what he hoped was just old red paint.

"Why do you think they hate me, Trip?" Michael asked. "It's exhausting, having demons and murderers on my tail no matter where I go."

Trip shrugged and looked up at the gruesome warning with a grim expression on her face. "I don't know. The whole good versus evil thing? The fact that they aren't very smart? I mean, it's not like they have a chance to beat us, not when you have that weird habit of coming back to life every time they try and off you. Maybe it's all some sort of messed up game caused by bored gods? Does it really matter what the reason is? Does it really matter why?"

"What the hell does that mean?"

"It means that there are three million and sixteen sons of bitches that want us both dead. Hell, I don't know! I'm just as lost as you are!" She crossed her arms around her stomach like she was trying to hold her guts in. "I just don't like wondering why when no matter what the reason, the result is still the same. We still have to bust our asses and get the hell kicked out of us so we can save the world or whatever, whether it's because of the gods or science or anything else. So why get hung up on the reasons, Michael? Why?"

He didn't have an answer for that. They stood in silence for a while, looking at the crude drawing in a silence that finally untensed.

Trip got closer to the drawing and said, "Who the hell is Spit Man?"

"Very funny," Michael said. "It's a nickname, Jackie Jackass."

"So they gave you a stupid nickname? Seems more like proof they can't spell. This will be a piece of cake. I doubt you'll die even once this time around." She looked back at him and tilted her chin defiantly, as if daring him to say that they wouldn't be perfectly fine.

Michael couldn't help the smile forming on his face.

She nudged him and tilted her head toward the pass. "It's now or never, Spirit Man."

Michael nodded, and they slowly made their way toward the main entrance. A gentle breeze brushed past and leaves of all colors snowed down around them. About half the leaves were in the shapes of snowflakes. It was a stunning sight as thousands of leaves drifted through the sky. Soon the leaves even blocked the sun from the sky.

Michael stopped and gazed in wonder. Where did these leaves even come from? So many leaves. So many dreams to catch in the wind. Who can catch the wind? Who can catch dreams and leaves? All of them kept slipping from his hands. No matter how he chased or jumped or clawed at them, they always would flutter, just beyond his grasp.

Soon everything around them became dark as the sun itself was blocked by the leaves. Trip grabbed his hand and they ran into the dark entrance of Satan's Pass. The only light came from the next neon sign that read, "Suck luck to you, Spit Man and Dream Stripper." This time they didn't so much as pause, both of them flipping it off with a giggle as they walked past. Better not to give such petty taunts even a moment of their time.

They made their way to Lost Causes Union Station.

Lost Causes. Just like our dreams and lives. Everyone seemed to be lost and confused about their own destiny. Man suffers while the gods turn a blind eye and laugh at all of the mere mortals. It didn't matter how much people dreamed, the little gods would shatter them. Making plans for the future, only for tragedy to strike and take us before our time.

What did it mean to be in Satan's Pass, heading to Lost Causes Union Station?

"What are we fighting for anyways?" Michael mused. "And who is the girl with the white stone? How can a little girl save the world? Maybe Bones was right. You can never change the world as it is. Full of misery, sorrow, pain and death."

Trip spun around and slapped him full force across his face with no warning. When his eyes cleared, he could see her shaking, tears running down her face. She jabbed a finger in his face and snarled, "Don't you ever think that way again, Michael. There are plenty of reasons to keep on fighting. We need to save the kids, our families, our future! We can't just give up. The world can change, a little at a time. You just, you just need to believe it can."

Michael touched his stinging cheek. Why was she reacting so strongly to what he said? What was the point of hope in all this darkness? Surely she could understand the hopelessness, the sense of being dragged down into the darkness. Sometimes it really did feel easier to just let the current take him.

But instead of voicing his thoughts, he stood still.

There was something in the air around him, something he couldn't put his finger on. It was dark and sticky, whispers in the back of his mind drifting in and out so fast that he could barely notice them. It felt like a blanket, pressing down around his mind, blocking out the light and somehow leaving him still cold.

"Trip, something is going on in this cave."

"There is nothing in this cave! If you are going to be a wimp and flake out on me then—"

"Shut up. Take a moment and think. Something is not right."

Michael closed his eyes. Sometimes the only way he could make sense of what he was seeing was to stop relying on his sight and look in another way, without eyes.

She paused, hands still shaking. She took in a deep breath and then another. With a tilt of her head, she said, "What is that? I can feel it now. Like...like being smothered." She cleared her throat as if to get more air to her lungs.

"I don't know. But we need to get out of here fast or who knows what will happen."

There was a blinding flash and a pop that echoed in the tunnel as spotlights focused in on them. Michael's eyes snapped open and immediately watered at the bright light, which made it hard to see around them.

Raven Bones stepped out of the shadows and started clapping. "Give the two idiots a round of applause. They figured it out before killing each other or themselves."

Trip and Michael stumbled to cover each other's backs, but through the blinding lights, they could see they were surrounded, a hundred Strikers all pointing guns right at them.

    DREAM OF THE SPIRIT MAN

Michael grinned. Now this was something he could deal with. He could fight the good fight, whatever that meant, and he would find the girl with three eyes that carried the white stone in her hands. Doubts he may have, but a battle? Battle had no place for doubt, and that was a very good thing.

Chapter 9

Trip pulled out the Deadly Eye from her pocket. It spun and shifted, snapping back into its original form. It floated, humming low as it shifted from one enemy to the next, but it didn't start yet. Was it waiting for something? Did their enemies have to start firing before it would work, or did it know something Michael didn't? Or worse, was there a chance that the strange weight of the cave was affecting the Deadly Eye as well?

Trip seemed to notice all this as well as she twisted one of her hands off. She frowned, surveying the army around them as if mentally imagining them all bursting into flames.

"Are you really going to try to fight us here?" General Bones asked, his nose in the air. "We have you surrounded. There is no possible way you can get out of here alive. Surrender and we may be kind enough to bring you to Lord Striker and let him rip your hearts out."

Michael rolled his eyes and barked a harsh laugh. "I've already done that. I've lain on the cold ground and felt my heart's blood drip onto my face, and I'm still here, dream and dream again. I've been killed so many times, what does it matter to me if you kill us here? We will just appear somewhere else, alive as ever, and you will continue on your fruitless quest to kill us." He spread his arms open wide. "So go ahead, try to kill us and we'll end up right back here again, ready to kick your ass through any number of deaths."

General Bones tilted his head, an obnoxious air of confidence coating the man. "Really? Well, that can be your answer. Are you so certain that the woman next to you would agree?"

"Of course," Michael said, but one glance at Trip and his certainty wavered. She had been so scared at the prospect of dying again when they were stranded on the bridge with the tank. Maybe her relationship with resurrection was different from his.

Her face was expressionless and hard, her eyes trained unblinkingly on Raven Bones, watching him like a snake watches a mouse.

Bones laughed. "It really doesn't look like it. Maybe I should let her break your fragile little heart before I rip it out and present it to Lord Striker."

Michael took a step back, still on edge, but looked at Trip. She was shaking through her entire body as if she was freezing. Her one attached hand rubbed at the stump where the other connected, her fingers tracing symbols Michael did not understand where her left hand rightfully belonged.

"Trip?" Michael asked.

She wouldn't look at him in the eyes and shook her head but she didn't say anything, still watching Raven Bones.

"Trip, are you not okay with dying for the right cause?" Michael asked.

She glared at him and said, "Of course not, stupid! Not everyone is the Spirit Man, you know. Who the fuck is okay with dying? I don't know how you are so calm about it either. Have you really died so many times that it has lost all impact on you? Do I really matter so little that you can just throw me aside, let me die? Oh, good old Trip, she'll just bounce back, what's a little horrible pain and dismemberment?"

"What are you talking about? Death doesn't matter in this world. It doesn't change anything," Michael protested.

Her eyes were full of hurt as she said, "It changes everything. How could you have not noticed? Every time you die, you change. You become a little less human, a little more...different." She shivered again, shaking her head. "Doesn't it bother you?"

"What are you talking about? What could it have changed?"

"You really don't remember me, do you? You don't remember anything." The disappointment and bitterness in her eyes shocked him.

Michael felt like he had been shot through the heart. In fact, he looked down just to make sure he hadn't been, but no clear wounds were seen on his body. He had met Trip before? That would explain why she felt so familiar, why interacting with her felt as natural as breathing. But what were they to each other then? And if they had known each other, why hadn't she given him some sort of indication before now?

General Bones laughed softly and said, "Oh, that really is the good stuff. Fill him with confusion, with doubt. Build his heart, only to break it."

Michael spun around, about to spew venomous words that he would surely regret, when Trip grabbed his arm and pulled him back to face her. "Look, Michael, of course I'm scared. Last time I played this high-stakes game, I lost everything I cared about. I lost Nevaeh and Noel. I lost my hands. I lost you. I don't want to go through that again."

Michael could swear he heard a thud near the back of the cave, but Trip reached out with her right hand and caressed his face, bringing it back towards hers.

She continued, "I can't stand to think that I will lose you again. I need you here, next to me. But if this is really our last moment together, and if you won't remember, then"—she pulled him closer, her lips mere inches from his own—"perhaps I will do what I've been wanting to from the moment I first saw you."

Michael closed his eyes and leaned in, wrapping his arms around her waist, pulling her closer still. Just before their lips locked, General Bones said, "Now!"

Michael tensed but the bullets never came. Trip pulled back and smiled up at Bones. "Did ya like our performance?"

Bones sputtered and shouted, "Now, you boneheads! Kill them."

Michael looked around, but the entire fleet was on the ground, blood pooling around their bodies, their heads all neatly separated from their necks.

General Bones sputtered as he looked at his troops. Trip grinned, her left hand flying back to her, along with a knife coated with blood. Wiping it off with a cloth, she said, "Really do need to watch both hands if you want to catch the magic trick as it is happening, Bones. Otherwise, things might just disappear from before your very eyes."

The Deadly Eye whirled and hummed, focusing its beam on General Bones. Trip pointed at Bones with her left hand and said, "Boom," as the laser erupted and cut Bones in half.

Chapter 10

The laser went off and the Deadly Eye folded itself up, landing neatly in Trip's hand.

"What just happened?" Michael asked, confused at how things changed around for their favor so quickly.

Trip held out her hand and Michael took it, barely able to keep his eyes off her as she practically skipped over the body of General Bones. Michael had really thought they were dead this time. He thought of the moment before he'd thought they were about to bite the dust, how she'd pressed against him, how close they'd come to… Well, not only to dying. "Was any of what you were saying true?" he asked, watching closely for her reaction.

She shrugged, not looking back at him, but her fingers tightened around his own.

Michael continued, "Because you really do feel familiar."

She stopped in her tracks and looked up at the ceiling. Her jaw was set hard, like she was keeping her jaw shut through a great effort of will. He waited for her to speak and after what felt like eons, she did.

"The best lies are mostly truth. Strange things really do happen when people here die. We become different. Take as much of what I said as true as you want." She sighed and looked at him, and he couldn't read the look that was in her eyes.

"So I do know you," Michael said slowly. "We've met, and I forgot you. I forgot everything we went through." Whatever that everything meant….He felt a churn of guilt in his gut. Whatever they'd been through before, whatever he couldn't remember, it had clearly left a serious mark on Trip. She began shaking at the notion of dying, even knowing that it wouldn't mean a permanent death. What must she have been through to get to that point? What had they

    DREAM OF THE SPIRIT MAN

been through together? He hated the idea that there were journeys that he couldn't remember. What else might he have forgotten?

She didn't say anything, so he went around in front of her and guided her face to look at him. Tears welled up in her eyes and she crashed into his chest, holding onto him like she never wanted to let him go. Almost like she didn't really believe he was there at all.

"You left me, you asshole!" she said into his chest, her voice thick with wetness. "You said you would help me, that you would protect me and the kids and help us survive, and then you just vanished into thin air. I thought I was never going to find you again. Do you know how many times I sent my hands through random portals, hoping that you were on the other side of one of them? Do you know what it's like to wonder if you even made it back? You're the Spirit Man, things work differently for you. But when I did hear of you again, it was almost worse. You were fine, helping people as you could. Finding your heart. You didn't go looking for us. You didn't care." She pulled back and glared at him. "You didn't even remember."

Michael squeezed her tight and kissed her forehead. "I am sorry. There is nothing I can do that can make this up, but that doesn't mean I won't try. But we are going to get into risky situations a lot. I can't promise that I won't die again."

In fact, Michael knew that if there was ever a moment where he had to choose between his life and Trip's, that he would save her, no matter what the cost. Even if he had to forget her again, that would be better than letting her face the death she feared so much. At least death was only a blip for him.

She choked out a laugh and said, "I know that, dummy. I just want you to be careful. I don't want you to forget me again. And I was be-ing truthful before. I am scared of dying. Just, please, don't go seek it out. I need you here. Your world needs you here."

Michael smiled, and Trip cleared her throat, stepping back, though she allowed their hands to remain intertwined. "We have got to get going. Death won't stay with Bones or his army for long and we got to get out before they have the chance to corner us again. And I know that disappearing trick won't work twice."

Michael nodded and turned to go down the path, Trip right next to him.

The cave continued through the mountain, winding up and down until they reached a place where the path branched off into four different directions. It was difficult to see down the different paths, and with Bones and his army surely pulling their guts back together behind them, they couldn't afford to waste time going down a dead end. "Where do you think we should go?" Michael asked.

Trip glared at him and said, "How the hell would I know, dumbass? Didn't I just say I don't have all the answers?" She sighed and looked around in the darkness. "Maybe we can find some sort of destiny clue. Isn't fate a whole part of your thing, Spirit Man?"

Michael chuckled and nodded. He closed his eyes, took a deep breath, and opened them again, trying to make himself believe that there would be something that would help them when he opened his eyes. Not exactly a prayer, but more faith in the world, in himself: he would be fine, because he had been fine in the past. Something would help him, because something always did.

He opened his eyes and looked around. Had it worked? Was anything different? There: a bright spot in the darkness of the tunnel. He saw that it was a piece of paper on the ground. It was a train schedule. He bent and picked it up, looking at it more closely.

According to this piece of paper, all trains were canceled except for one that read, "The Land of Enchantment departs Tuesday at 8:35 A.M." New Mexico? But how did this land connect back to his home state back in the other world? It didn't make any sense.

There was something in the other entries for the train schedules. "Satan Claus" was in faded letters. Did the people of this world have a Christmas? And what did that imply? Or was this just a world where things got lost and it didn't matter what they meant in their original worlds?

"What's that?" Trip asked, looking at the paper in his hand. He held it to her and she peered at it, frowning. "Any idea what this is supposed to mean?"

He shook his head, and then a random thought came to him. With all his time traveling, he'd learned to trust his random thoughts. "Do you have the plastic eyeball Atlas gave you, Trip?" he asked.

Trip looked at him like he had grown a third eye but felt around in her pockets, pulling it out gingerly between the very tips of her thumb and forefinger, like if it touched her for too long, she'd never be able to get the feeling of eyeball off. She grimaced and said, "Yeah. Why? Do you want to hold it? Cause it is super gross. I'm happy for this thing to be your problem now."

Michael nodded and put the eye up to his own. Through the plastic eye, he saw millions of butterflies flying around, dancing in the cave like neon lights overlaid in his vision. They came from the direction they went and swirled around where Trip and Michael stood, finally twisting out into only one of the four paths. He was about to put away the plastic eye when he noticed something. Each butterfly had eyes on their wings. Sometimes they seemed painted on, flat and unmoving, but then he'd blink and they'd blink back like living eyes, darting back and forth and then staring at him.

He handed the eye back to Trip, who caught it in a piece of her shirt before she put it back in one of her pockets. "Don't tell me that gross thing actually helped you decide which path we should take," she said, wiping her hands off on his back with a sound of disgust.

"Well, if we are to follow the butterflies, then we go down the second path."

She looked at him like his third eye gained a brother and said, "According to the butterflies. Did you hit your head recently or something? Because if you are going crazy, it would be nice to get a heads up about it now."

"Of all the strange things in this world," Michael said, "butterflies are the ones that confuse you?"

"Visible butterflies are one thing, but invisible butterflies that can only be seen through Atlas' plastic eye? Yah, that is a bit of a stretch."

He grinned and reached out his hand, saying, "Well, do you have any other ideas?"

She rolled her eyes but took his hand. "Fine. We'll follow your damn butterflies." As they began to walk down the path, she bumped her hip against his. "And don't think I'm forgetting that you stuck me with carrying the gross thing again, either."

Michael's laugh echoed down the path ahead, making the way ahead seem just a little bit lighter.

Chapter 11

After another bit of walking, Michael asked, "If we become less human every time we die, what happens when the bad guys die and come back? Are they changed by it, too?"

"The same thing. Less human. More monstrous. A bit more stupid, if you ask me, but that one's just my pet theory."

Michael paused, something about all of this bothering him a bit. "Trip, please, just tell me."

She looked at him, her gaze unreadable. "Tell you what?"

"Don't be that way, Trip. I know there are things you're holding back about how this world works, about how you work in it. Please."

Trip turned to Michael and said, "You want a full history of this world, of all the worlds that are connected to it? You want to know why the leaves fall from the trees or why we don't really die? Go become a scientist. We are Trues. Visionaries. Heroes. Do your job and let them do theirs."

"Trip, if I am to try to save the worlds, I need to know how things work. I need to know the rules. Please, Trip. I know you know something you aren't telling me."

"I know lots I'm not telling you. I know eons." Her voice was icy and distant. Something about this line of questioning made her shut him out, and he had no idea why.

They walked a bit in silence for a while, following the path through Satan's Path in silence. He wasn't sure what point there was to holding things back from him, but Trip was a smart woman, and if there was something he needed to know, he trusted that she'd figure out a way to tell him.

They'd been walking in silence down the path for about ten minutes when Trip suddenly stopped and said, "Fine. You want to know how things work here? Hardly anyone here was actually born here.

Nevaeh and Noel are the only other people I know besides myself who are still around that were actually from here. Everyone else just appeared one day, like you did. Their forms and such relied on what they believed before they moved over. Or they just appeared because the people here believed that they would. There were a lot of studies done about it, but everything was lost when Striker appeared. Chaos reigned, and we lost a lot of our history that day. A long with a lot of lives. Dying was rarer before those days, so we had no idea what the deaths would mean. At first it was simple, but the changes happened and caught us off guard. Do you really think that we were the only Visionaries to begin with? Each death changed people, twisted them into something else. Something that didn't care about life or death. Almost every Striker, Savior, or general was a Visionary to begin with. But after a while, people lose hope. Or something. We didn't know what caused it, and before we knew it, we couldn't study it anymore. There was just too many of them. And they wouldn't stop until all hope was chased out of this world or any world." She shrugged her shoulders. "I guess that's what I know. Happy now?"

"That's a lot of information to drop on me all at once. But if you knew that, why didn't you tell me sooner?" Michael asked.

Trip's hands clenched and she said, "Hope is what keeps you—you. It's what makes sure you come back. There is a reason why we adopted the title 'Trues' after the first wars started. We were some of the last Visionaries to remain true to ourselves. True to what our beliefs are, that good must triumph over evil."

"So everyone we've been fighting have been on our side at one time? Even the death birds and bat demons?"

Trip shook her head, "No. Those two were one of the kinds that were here before this all happened. And I'm sure they have something to do with how this whole thing got caused, but I don't know how. And most of the regular people think they are relatively safe in their cities, but the armies of evil will target them as soon as they get rid of the rest of us. And the regular people will be defenseless without hope. Everyone needs hope. I thought that if you didn't know that you could change into one of them, then maybe you wouldn't. But the deaths still affect you. Even our hero is vulnerable."

Michael looked down at his shoes, lost in thought. "I don't know if anything I say can make you worry less, but I will try to be more careful. I won't give up. I need to do my part. Even if it ends up being small in the end. Or if it ends up with everything gone. I have to try. That's the least I can do, right?"

Trip put one hand on her hip. "Now don't go assuming you're the only one willing to die. That one part actually was an act. Sure, death scares me, but that doesn't mean it's not worth the risk for something I believe in. I just…I need you to know the risks."

Michael held out his hand. After a moment of hesitation, Trip smiled and took it in hers.

"As long as I remember you, I will fight to make it back to your side," Michael vowed. The words hung in the air as if they were physical objects, heavy and real. He wasn't sure how he knew it, but the promise meant something in this world, and it mattered that he'd made it.

Red rushed up Trip's face and she tried to turn around, but Michael kept a gentle grip on her hand as he continued, "And I hope that if I do forget, that you will drag me right back to your side once again. We will find a way to fix this before we lose ourselves. I promise, Dream Tripper."

Trip clasped his hand in hers and brought it to the level of her eyes. "I promise, Spirit Man." For a moment they stood there, looking into each other's eyes, and Michael was sure that this moment was one he could never forget.

The spell broken, and Trip laughed, letting their hands drop. "Come on, there is plenty of time where we can be all serious and depressed later. Right now, we got to get out of this cave and find Nevaeh and Noel. I'm sure that that's our next step."

Michael grinned and let her lead the way. No matter what would happen, he was sure he would never break his promise.

<h1 style="text-align:center">Chapter 12</h1>

They walked through the narrow, dark tunnels for what felt like must have been ages before Trip and Michael emerged into a large space, filled with toppled benches and old train tracks. Flames leapt from dirty gray and green trash cans, burning a noxious fume that clogged the air and made it hard to see or breathe. In the patches of the smoke, Michael could see shadows moving this way and that, faster than he could really track. Light filtered down from the cracks in the ceiling, its streaks clearly visible in the rising smoke.

"What's here?" Michael asked, trying to figure out if the flickers in the corner of his vision were real or not.

"We're in Lost Causes Central Station. What do you think is here?" Trip snapped.

"Lost Causes? But that's just a name. Besides, we are here too, right?"

"Things aren't always what they seem. Thought you knew that much about this land, but I guess even a great hero can be stupid at times."

Michael rolled his eyes and said, "I've been to lots of places, it's hard to know everything about everywhere."

"Oh, sure," Trip said, "And my hands don't come flying off to slit the throats of unsuspecting Strikers."

"Are you going to answer my question or not?"

She turned around and grinned, walking backwards for a bit, when her smile dropped. She grabbed Michael's shirt and dove down to the ground just as machine gun fire tore apart the ground that was behind them.

Trip put a finger to her lips and slipped further into the smoke and Michael joined her.

Raven Bones stepped out of the tunnel, the giant hole in his chest stitching itself up with every second. He lifted his head high and shouted, "Come on out, Michael! Fight me! I beg you, oh mighty Spirit Man! Let's play! We didn't get a fair match last time, after all, with all your dirty tricks!"

The room echoed oddly, spreading his voice far and wide and making it sound like he was jumping out of every shadow.

A small group of Strikers and Saviors gathered around Bones with an uncertain number behind them; Michael couldn't tell how many had come back and could only see the shapeless mass of bodies pressing out through the tunnel behind them.

"Michael!" Bones screamed over and over again. "Come out, you coward, and fight me like the Spirit Man you claim to be!"

Michael saw a flash of blue out of the corner of his eye. Was that Trip transforming into her ultimate fighting gear? Or was it one of the shadows playing tricks on him? He had a uniform too, didn't he? He closed his eyes and focused, a royal blue outfit covered with eyes appearing on his body. He blinked once and then again and his vision focused, peering past most of the smoke.

Bones shouted, "All of these battles and raging wars for what? A little god who is worse than a ghost! She doesn't exist. You are a blind fool who can't change a damn thing, Spirit Man. Forget this world! You can't even help your own. The world doesn't want to be changed and will snap back no matter what you try to do. You should know that by now."

Michael stepped out of the smoke, noticing without looking that the eyes lifted off of his battle gear, aiming at the enemies before him. A long futuristic looking gun materialized in his hands and he pointed it right at Bones.

"Charge him!" Bones commanded. "Kill those damn fools and find Trip before she can do any more damage. Nobody can change the world. It ain't worth much anyways."

The small group split into two, one charging Michael and one disappearing into the fog. Michael worried about Trip but knew she could take care of herself. He had his own battle he had to worry about. Not to mention that Trip would probably rip his head off and

shove it straight up his ass if he died here because he was more focused on her safety than on winning the fight.

The small army that charged him consisted of about twenty-five
creatures carrying a mix of guns, swords, and axes. Michael picked
up his gun and started shooting, trusting the eyes on his back
to guard him from what he couldn't see. Bright red laser beams
erupted out of the gun and found its target with each shot. He spun,
hitting a Striker that was aiming for his back, just as the eyes on his
shoulders erupted in a laser show of their own. Within seconds, all
the soldiers after him were dead. With their noise gone, he could
just see flashes of blue and the cries as enemy after enemy hit the
ground, destroyed by the Spirit Man's assault.

"You okay, Trip?" Michael yelled over the chaos of the battle.

"Perfect! Never better! Practically a vacation!" Trip shouted back.

Her voice echoed, but even with the distortion, he could hear the
pain in her voice, the gritted teeth of someone fighting to keep it
together through the pain. He looked for her in the chaos, and as if
by magic, she appeared from the smoke, holding onto her right arm.

Michael began to run over to her, but froze when he noticed Bones
was watching them with an impassive expression on his cruel face.

Trip straightened and removed her hand from her wound, pointing the gun in her hand at his hand. "Come on, you ass! Show us
what you got!"

Michael put up his hand and said, "What is it that you want from
us, Bones? Why are you doing all this, why cause all this senseless
violence and death?"

"I want you dead, Spirit Man!" Bones screamed. "Dead, dead,
dead!"

Michael and Trip waited for him to make the next move as his
screams turned to howls and filled up their ears and scratched their
minds. Michael fell to his knees, clawing at his ears as visions flared
past his eyes, too many to pick out anything more specific than images and confusion. So many hearts drained of blood, rushing like a
river through the land. So many eyes torn out in the name of "hope."
Many eyeless faces crying blood instead of tears down silent

     DREAM OF THE SPIRIT MAN

shrieking faces. Gods and goddesses hearing prayers and ignoring the pleas of their people. He couldn't process all of it, all the waves of grief and anger and pain and loss, hate and rage and violence and death. It washed over him in a great, nearly overpowering rush, and he struggled to stay upright as the visions flooded his mind's eye.

Michael felt a hand on his shoulder and blinked, wiping all the sights away from his vision, even as he knew he would never be able to unsee those visions. They would be with him forever now; he felt it as surely as he felt anything else.

General Raven Bones cried out again, a wordless cry of rage, but Trip anchored Michael in the world with a hand on his elbow, a concerned look.

The room fell silent and Raven Bones started laughing, cackling mad. His awful mirth echoed from the very walls of the room. "Spirit Man, do you know anything about the cause you fight for?" His voice was impossibly quiet and loud at the same time. "Do you know what horrors the Visionaries that you save have done in the name of freedom? Of hope? Did you know, once you give up, death doesn't hurt anymore? Does it keep you up at night, the way your old wounds ache in a way you can never scratch? That's because this body you're wearing now wasn't even the one that got hurt! Give up and join us. Die one more time and die for Lord Striker. Wipe this land of the foolishness that has plagued it for far too long. Aren't you ready, finally, to receive your restful reward?"

Michael took a deep breath and stood up. He stared Bones in the eyes and was about to say something when Trip spoke first.

"No side is perfect," she said, steel in her voice. "But that doesn't mean that we shouldn't try. Try to fix what we did, to help heal the broken worlds."

Bones tilted his head and said, "And no one knows how much the Visionaries broke it like you do, Trip."

She stood silent. Michael put his hand on her shoulder and said, "We cannot change the past. We can only try to fix the future. Everyone has done things they aren't proud of. Trust me. But we can improve and repent and heal."

Bones glared at them, a giant black sword slowly growing in his hand. "I see you aren't quite ready to see things my way. Perhaps a few more deaths for you and the ones you love will change your mind?" He grinned savagely. "I'll be happy to be your teacher in another lesson in loss, oh Spirit Man."

He leapt up, swinging his sword right towards them and Michael barely got his gun up in time to block it. Sparks flew each way as Bones aggressively attacked, swinging again and again until Michael was at the edge of the tracks.

His improved vision faded, going back to normal. He blinked hard but couldn't afford to give Raven Bones a single moment of leeway. Every opening was pounced on, and if he didn't keep on his toes, he'd lose quickly.

Maybe he was just too tired at this point. Was there ever a time here in the dream worlds when he wasn't fighting? For his life, for the lives of others, for hope itself? Had he had a chance to truly rest since he got here? He had to focus. He had to rely on someone else.

"Trip! Help!"

"What can I do? You've got a gun and can barely hold him off! All I got is a small knife," Trip yelled from the sidelines, nervously hopping from foot to foot.

"Focus!" Michael shouted again, dodging the strike that would have taken off his head for certain if he didn't react immediately. Even having the conversation with Trip might take too much of his concentration.

"What are you talking about?" she yelled, looking around. She growled in frustration and caught eye of her royal blue uniform with all the weird eyes on her body.

Suddenly, a couple hundred bolts of lasers shot out of the strange looking eyes. These eyes rose and pointed at Bones and struck him point blank, slamming into him with enough force to make him stagger. Michael dodged out of the way as the shots exploded one after another. Bones lunged toward him but the shots held him back until he was blasted to smithereens, leaving nothing but a black smear on the ground behind him.

Michael sank to the ground and looked up at the sky. "Sarah, God, or whoever is up there, listen, you have to hear me out. Mind if we can have a tiny break? Pretty please?"

Trip laughed. Her arms wrapped around herself as tears of relief dripped down her face.

Grinning at her, Michael added, "I might even consider actually praying now and then!"

He got to his feet, groaning on his way up. Every part of him ached, but he had to check on Trip. Something was bleeding and he had to make sure she didn't die on him. He saw the smudge that was Bones and kicked at it again. "He'll be back."

Trip rested her head on his shoulder and said, "Shush. We survived. That's what matters right now."

He smiled and then held his hand inches from the skin on her arm. "Can I see it?"

She shrugged, "I've had worse. This certainly ain't going to kill me."

He nodded and said, "I'd still like to check."

She rolled her eyes but offered her arm, flinching slightly when he brushed over the wound. It was about two inches long, but pretty shallow. "It looks fine. As long as they aren't starting to poison their blades or anything, you should be fine. But I'd still like to clean it and wrap it with something."

His normal clothes reappeared and he ripped a bit of the bottom of his shirt, wrapping it around her arm tightly. He'd had to do a fair bit of first aid over the years, and he was glad to have the chance to show Trip that he would do his best to help care for her and stick by her now that they had found each other again.

Michael stepped back to admire his work when he saw Trip's face was bright red and that she pointedly looked away from him.

He got closer and said, "My dream girl."

She jerked to him, face somehow even redder, and rolled her eyes. "Oh, come on. We really should get going. We don't know when he'll be back."

Michael laughed, an honest laugh. So, flattery made Trip nervous?

He had to test out how far it could go. "I really am lucky to be on an adventure with the prettiest fighter there is."

Trip turned on her heel and stomped off, but not before Michael spotted the way her eyebrows shot straight up, her eyes growing wide as she quickly covered up her emotions again. She strode away from him down the path, not looking at him. "You wouldn't say that if you knew some of the things I have done. Bones was right. I don't know what I am doing, trying to fix things. There is nothing I can do that can—"

Michael grabbed her left hand and she stopped, still facing forward. "Trip, I don't care what you did. Are you trying to do better?"

"Yes but—"

"Have you tried to repair what you did?"

"Every day. But—"

"Then you are good in my eyes. Look, we can't change what we did. Everyone can be pretty awful people at one point or another, simply because they don't know better or because they don't know all of the details. Did you murder an innocent?"

"No."

"Then you have nothing to worry about. I won't judge you for what you might have done in your past. I like you for who you are now."

She turned to him, her eyes wide, filled with the beginnings of tears. "You don't know. You say that now, but—"

"I promised I would never leave you. Nothing you tell me can change my mind. I know you, Dream Tripper. You are a good person. I just wish you could see yourself the way I see you."

Trip stood frozen, a look of faint surprise on her face.

He closed the distance between them, and she reached up and touched his cheek.

"I don't know what I did to deserve running into you. Thank you."

Trip turned around and marched on without another word.

Chapter 13

They followed the butterflies outside, relieved they made it without another great battle. They only had so much energy, and they had to walk on foot to their next destination. Right at the side of the building next to the two swinging doors was a Change Machine. It looked more like a pinball machine than a change machine, but it did have the words "Change" in bright neon letters on the top of it. A man dressed in a janitor uniform was busy putting in coins and pulling back the plunger only to watch the ball fall in the hole at the bottom without even trying to operate the flippers. There was a big black leather bag full of random objects right by his feet. One of the clearest objects in the bag was a director's clapperboard with smudged words written in chalk.

Instantly Michael recognized who this man was.

"Lohman!"

Lohman glanced up from his game and went to shake Michael's hand. "Hello, Michael. How are you?"

Lohman radiated an energy of quiet benevolence, like a king surveying a kingdom, no matter what uniform he was wearing, and Michael had really looked up to him when they'd met before, in other worlds and times.

"Pretty good, I guess, but that hardly matters right now. What are you doing here?" Michael responded, feeling the strong grip in his hand even when Lohman let go.

Lohman's head slid toward the bag by the machine and ran a hand through his hair. "Well, to be honest, I was going to swoop in and save you."

Trip crossed her arms and said, "Really? With an amateur movie maker kit designed for five-year-olds?"

Lohman shifted his weight to one side and walked over to Trip, picking up a piece of her hair and sniffing it in a quick movement. He disappeared just as Trip swung her arm and appeared a few feet away with his arms crossed, imitating her body language for a few seconds before bursting into a huge smile. "You must be the lovely Dream Tripper! Michael has told me all about you."

Trip rolled her eyes, "Oh please. He didn't even remember me moments ago. How in the world would he have the chance to talk about me?"

"Time is a funny thing. I forget you humans or humanoids or whatever it is you are calling yourselves lately have a more linear relationship with time. Time and I don't really get along. Beginning, end, middle, what does it matter to me?"

"Are you saying you're some kind of time traveler?" Trip said, clearly skeptical. She looked at Michael with an expression of simultaneous disbelief and indignation.

Michael put his hand on Trip's shoulder and said, "Calm down, Trip. Lohman and I go way back."

Lohman smiled and bowed, tilting his head just as he was rising. "Well, 'way back' is a bit of an overstatement. And understatement. But that is true."

Trip closed her eyes and took a deep breath. She unraveled her arms and looked at him. "I guess it's good to see an old friend of Michael's. You still haven't answered my question yet. What's with the movie stuff?"

"It was going to be hilarious. I was going to spring in when things were looking bad in your last battle and cry, 'Cut.' I was going to make this whole thing seem like it was just a part of a movie set and that gullible Bones would have bought it. But I suppose I got a bit distracted. Pity."

Michael twisted, trying to see how the machine Lohman was at before worked. It wasn't quite like anything he had ever seen before. "What is this machine, anyway?"

"I thought you would never ask!" Lohman boomed with a grin. "This here is the Change Machine. Get a high score and have the chance to change the world. But all I get are these silly 'I owe you' notes back. It really is terrible."

"How do you know if you have a high score? It didn't really look like you were doing anything?" Trip said, her eyes suspicious as she looked over the machine.

Lohman smiled and walked over to the machine, pulling out a quarter from his pocket and handing it to Michael. "Why don't you give it a shot, eh?" he asked with a devilish grin.

Michael put the coin in the machine and he was pulled into the game. Images flashed rapidly, one action leading to the next and to something else, but it was gone before he could even understand what he was seeing.

Michael stumbled back, rubbing his eyes, which were still seeing the after images of whatever the machine had shown him. Lohman patted him on the back and laughed. "You did better than I thought at your first try, Spirit Man. Only time can tell whether that did anything, though, and as I said before, time is an asshole."

Trip cleared her throat and said, "Well, if you boys are done playing with your machine, we have a mission to complete, world to save, all that little stuff."

Lohman went over to the wall and slouched against it, a slight smile on his face. He said, "Which mission are you referring to? Maybe I can help."

"We are looking for Noel and Nevaeh," Trip said slowly. "That's the big thing."

Lohman waved his hand and shook his head, "You'll figure that out soon enough. Now, what are you truly seeking? What is it that your hearts desire?"

Trip's mouth opened and shut again. She couldn't think of anything.

Michael answered instead and said, "We are looking for the girl with the white stone. Do you know where we can find her?"

"The road is long and winding. And the lights along the way can be bright and blinding."

Trip fought the urge to roll her eyes and said, "What does that mean?" Michael could tell from her tone that she was doing her best to stay patient.

Lohman shrugged and said, "I can't tell you where she is, but I can tell you that she is. Don't you worry your little heads. Sarah Eyestone is real. Annoyingly real at times."

Stunned, Michael stared into Lohman's eyes and tried to find any hint that the man in front of him was lying. "Is that her real name? Sarah Eyestone?"

"Sarah 'The Precious One' Eyestone," Lohman replied. "She might as well be a ghost though, Michael. No one has seen her in person for over three thousand years."

Trip said, "That's a long time. Do you have any idea what might bring her out? She is the only one powerful enough to fix things."

"The winding long road awaits you. Oh, where your journeys will lead. I'm almost jealous."

"Focus, Magic Man," Trip growled. "What can you tell us that is actually helpful?"

Lohman beamed at her and said, "Well, my dear, everything I've said will be useful at one point or another. But I think I know the true intent behind your question. You worry for your young charges and wish to know if your quest to reunite with them will be successful or not. Well, worry less. They have proven themselves capable of taking care of each other. Follow the road by the tracks and you will find them."

Michael asked, "What are you going to do then, Lohman?"

"I've got one hell of a mess to clean up in there, but I might just keep trying my luck at this machine here. You never know. Might just get lucky one day and hit the high score, changing the world for good."

Michael nodded and Lohman waved.

Fifteen minutes later, the ground beneath them changed from a black paved road to bricks as far as they could see.

"Seems like your friend was right," Trip said.

"He's always right. But what are you talking about? I don't see the kids quite yet."

"The road is a long and winding one."

Michael laughed and took her hand, knowing that their future was going to be an interesting one indeed.

Chapter 14

Golden red leaves fell from the sky as Michael and Trip followed the yellow bricks. They walked for mile after mile as the sun beat into their skin. Yet the sky was clear and shone blue. There were no bat demons chasing them or death birds wanting to tear into their skin and hearts. Michael was tired of the fighting and it felt good for a bit of peace, even though it might end at any moment. Even though he should have been hungry or thirsty by now, he was content to just walk down this path and take in the sights.

They walked and walked until they reached another sign by the edge of the road. It read, "Welcome to Least Heaven."

Michael thought that the sign should read, "East Heaven," but many strange things happened in this world. Maybe it wasn't a mistake as much as something else.

Michael stopped, and Trip soon followed. She looked on as he examined the sign. If he was honest, he kind of liked the L in front of the word east. "Aren't we all children under a less powerful god in the least heaven?" he murmured to himself.

Trip crouched in the shade of the sign and said, "Shouldn't we get going? That weirdo of yours said we were getting close to the kids and I really would like to see them. I need to make sure they are alright." She wrapped her arms around herself and rocked onto her heels, bouncing a little bit. Michael wasn't sure he'd ever seen her so happy before.

Michael held the eye that Atlas gave them to his eye and saw the butterflies were swarming in place, circulating around them in a flash of every color.

"I think we need to stay here," Michael said.

Trip groaned. "Why? We are so close to them I can feel it!"

"Maybe that's why we shouldn't move. If we are looking for the kids and they are looking for us, isn't there a chance we might miss them? Besides, the butterflies aren't moving."

"Well, it could be because you decided to stop moving. Which caused which?"

Michael sat next to her on the sand, taking her hand in his own. "Trip, I know you are worried, but this is what we need to do right now. We will find them. I promise."

Trip ripped her hand out of his grasp and said, "Well what about my promise?"

Michael didn't know what to say. The silence seemed to weigh on her and she sighed. "I promised them, Michael. I promised them that I would always be there for them when they needed me. What if they got hurt? What if they're cold, or scared, or hurt, and I'm out here taking my sweet time getting to them so I can protect them again?"

Michael reached out his hand again and she paused before taking it. Michael looked up at the great expanse of sky above them and said, "It's hard to know exactly what you need to be doing. It's even harder with kids 'cuz you want to help, but you never really know if it will help in the end or not. But let me tell you this, if they are anything like you, they are going to be okay."

She smiled ever so slightly, but it was enough to make his heart grow warm. What was it about this girl that made him want to do anything he could to see her smile? How was something so simple so important?

Dust billowed up the road in front of them and Trip jumped to her feet. Her clothing shifted to her warrior outfit in an instant, but the eyes stayed closed.

"I don't think whoever is coming is a threat," Michael said, slowly dusting himself off as he got off the ground.

"How can you be sure?" Trip asked but Michael didn't answer.

A dirt bike with a side car came pulling up, stopping right next to them. The bike was blue and gold and one kid was driving it while another was in the sidecar. The bike barely came to a stop when the one driving pushed down the kickstand and ran over to them, tossing his helmet off and wrapping his arms around Trip.

   DREAM OF THE SPIRIT MAN

After a long sweet moment, Trip pulled away and held his face in her hands, turning it slightly this way and that. "Noel! Are you okay? Have you been eating well? Where is Nevaeh?"

Noel smiled and gestured to the side car. "My sis is in there."

Trip ran over as the other kid took off her helmet. Memories burned behind Michael's eyes and he shook his head, trying to get them to come out. A memory flickered past his head and he caught a glimpse of something. Trip and what looked like two boys. But Noel just said sis. What did that mean?

Noel rolled his eyes. "Don't have your brain explode, Spirit Man. You made a mistake last time and we didn't feel like we trusted you enough to correct you at the time. But it was bugging her, so I promised that we would get you caught up if we met again. But mess with her and I will shred you to pieces, no matter how powerful everyone says you are."

Michael blinked and nodded. "Okay, fair enough," he said. Sure, he didn't really remember much, if anything, of their interaction before but he didn't want either of the twins to feel uncomfortable because of him. If he'd been mistaken about the other child's gender before, at least he could get it right now that he'd been corrected.

He walked over to the side car and tried to hide a laugh when Noel trailed him, arms crossed.

Trip broke apart from their hug and said, "Why are you still in the sidecar? Are you okay? What happened?"

Nevaeh looked away and Michael said, "The kids drove a long way. We should give them a bit of a break." He could sense the weariness like it was radiating off them. They must have come a terribly long way to find themselves here with Michael and Trip.

Nevaeh shook her head and said, "No. It's okay. I need to talk about it anyways. Noel, can you help me out?"

Noel pulled up the seat cover on the dirt bike and pulled out way more than should have ever fit in there, including a table, several folding chairs, and even a picnic basket. Finally, he pulled out a full-sized wheelchair and set it on the ground next to his sister. Ever so carefully, he picked her up and moved her over to the wheelchair.

Trip gasped but it took Michael a bit to understand what he was seeing. Her legs were missing parts, specifically the knees and ankles. The rest of the leg just kind of floated where it would normally belong, looking as alive as ever, except for the fact that it wasn't attached by flesh and bone.

"What happened?" Trip said, stopping inches from touching where Nevaeh's knees should have been. Her hands hovered like she wanted to do something, but she wasn't sure what.

Nevaeh sighed and said, "That is one very long story. Noel, do you mind doing the talking for a bit?"

He nodded and patted his sister's back. Noel said, "We've been hanging out in the Land of Sun. The Moon Queen decided to take us in for a bit and help us out 'cuz she never had kids of her own. Or that's what she would say. Right in front of her own children. No wonder she was killed. Anyways, the Sun King is sick and keeps talking about dying and if that happens, there will be no more sunlight in the entire land. We need your help to go fix him up."

Nevaeh rolled her eyes like Noel was missing the point. "Well, that too," she said. "But the asshole that killed the queen was also the asshole that stole parts of my legs. Said he would burn them if we tried to help the Sun King. But if you come with us, we won't be the ones helping the Sun King, so hopefully my legs will be safe if we're not the ones helping..."

"You will be," Noel finished for her, looking to Michael and Trip with a solemn nod.

Trip looked like she could bring down an entire army by herself singlehandedly at the moment, her expression furious and deadly. "Who threatened you? I will rip their tongue out and shove it up their ass before cutting out their eyes one by one and feeding them to the birds. Then I—"

Nevaeh rolled her eyes. "I don't really care what you do to him. I just want to save the country. And get my legs back if I can. And if anyone can save the Sun King, it's the mighty Dream Tripper and the great Spirit Man. Right?"

Her eyes opened wide she smiled. Trip groaned and rubbed

between her eyes. "No need to try and butter us up, kiddo. But I think Michael and I need to talk first."

Noel shrugged and said, "Whatever. It's about nighttime anyways. Might as well set up camp."

Michael turned toward the bright blue sky and asked, "Nighttime? What are you talking about?"

"Didn't we just say we were working on saving the Sun King?" Noel said. "This is his kingdom. The sun doesn't really move here. It's just how much light depending on how close you are to him. Right now, 'cuz he is suicidal, the closer you get to the capital, the darker it gets. It's perpetual twilight over the castle walls."

"But that can't be good for the land. What about crops and such? Sleep? All those things need the days and nights," Michael said. He could wrap his head around a lot of things, but a land with absolutely no night or day was beyond him.

Noel simply shrugged again. "Guess that means you should fix it soon, huh?" he said with a devilish grin.

Michael chuckled and couldn't help but agree, and for a while the four of them walked through the land, quiet and intent on the destination ahead.

Later, when they finally decided to stop for the night, Trip pulled Michael aside to talk with him. The kids were talking in hushed voices over the firepit, which felt a bit out of place in the blazing weather, but it kept them busy, and who knew what sort of creatures they'd need to stave off with its flames.

"I know I said I would help you if you helped me find the kids, but this is important." Trip said, once she was certain the kids couldn't hear what she was saying.

"The fate of this world and my world is in the hands of the girl with three eyes. We need to find her," Michael whispered back.

"I know, I know. But there has got to be a balance. I'm not even sure the girl with three eyes really exists. I've been in this land for a really long time and I haven't seen her. Anything that can be done, we must do ourselves. Which I think means helping the Sun Kingdom."

"I agree that they need help."

"Good, so you'll come?" Trip said, her face almost glowing.

Dang it, that wasn't what he meant. But she looked so hopeful. "Look, you are the one who tells me to be careful about how many times I die. Shouldn't I focus all of my energy on the ultimate goal of fixing things?"

Her expression wavered. "What's the point of saving the world if all the small things that make life worth living are gone? I understand if you won't go with us. But I'm going. I can't just stand by when there are people who need my help. Especially when they're those two kids."

She sighed and said, "I won't judge you for whatever decision you make. Just make sure you feel it's the right one." She walked a bit back to the fire pit and the sign when she paused and turned. "We are leaving in the morning. I'd really like it if you came."

Michael sat on the outskirts for a while and tried to think things through. To be honest, he didn't really need that much time, but he didn't want to look weak willed in front of Trip and the kids either. He had to at least give the appearance of thinking long and hard about this decision, even if it was already made in his gut long ago.

After waiting a bit, he walked back to camp with a small smile. "All right. I'm coming with. I want to do what I can."

Trip crashed into his arms, holding him tight. She was almost squealing with how happy she was and in that moment, he knew he made the right choice.

Chapter 15

It was hard to rest that night as the sun blazed high in the sky. The twins pulled out sleeping mats out of the dirt bike and fell asleep with ease, curling around each other like two peas in a pod. Trip got out and set up her own sleeping mat and fell asleep quickly as well. She looked almost like an angel when she slept, her expression smoothed over into complete peace in slumber. All that left Michael were his own thoughts. Was it safe to sleep at the moment? Who knew what could happen? What if the demons and strikers caught up to them?

The worries flooded his mind, but his body's exhaustion began to win out over his nerves. Eventually, he fell asleep as well.

The night passed without incident, and he woke up to the wonderful smell of bacon on the fire. Trip and the kids were already eating, quietly discussing plans for their trip into the Sun Kingdom.

"That's why the girl with the white stone is so important to him," Trip was saying. "I figure if we happen to get any closer to finding out where she is, then we should jump on it."

Michael stretched and waved to the Trues as he approached them.

Trip stopped talking and smiled softly towards him, handing him a plate full of food. "Morning."

"Didn't think that sleeping would help that much, but it did good."

Nevaeh nodded and said, "Rest is important. Even if we technically can go for weeks without rest, sleep is good for rejuvenating."

"So," Michael said in between shoveling bites of food down his throat, "what's the plan?"

Trip said, "The kids know where to go, so I figure we can just follow them."

"Isn't there a bit of an issue with that though? We don't have a ride and that bike can't hold all four of us."

Noel stuck out his tongue and said, "Duh. We have an extra dirt bike in the bag."

Michael turned and looked at the dirt bike and shook his head, "There is no way that you fit a whole dirt bike in there. It's just not possible."

Noel rolled his eyes. "We're Trues. We aren't bound by what you would consider possible. 'Sides, you have to put it together first."

Noel took off the seat and started pulling out tires, engine pieces, parts of the body, and more. Soon there was a good-sized pile of random parts.

Trip started to put it together while Michael wolfed down the rest of his food. After he was done, he got down and helped put it together. When it was all said and done, it was actually slightly bigger than the kids' dirt bike and had two seats. Noel shrugged when Trip asked about it and said, "Figured you guys needed more room, being adults and all. Don't think too much on it."

They ate again and set off, Trip holding on tight while Michael drove.

The band of Visionaries traveled along the yellow road for days before the road finally ended. As the dirt bike rolled to a halt, Michael and Trip looked around to see where they had ended up. They were right in front of a large empty parking lot with one solitary white building in the middle. The building was a one-story building complex with four huge glass windows in the front. Small black letters on the top read, "White Stone Factory."

The whole place seemed to be isolated and empty. A chill ran down Michael's spine as if someone was watching them, but he could sense no actual person anywhere nearby. What was causing that feeling?

"Why are we stopping here, Noel?" Michael asked.

The boy shook his head and Trip said, "Where is everybody?"

Nevaeh muttered, "Get ready."

Without warning, a strong wind blew in from out of nowhere. Within a few minutes, a huge grayish purple cloud rolled in the sky directly over them. The huge cloud blocked the sun and everything grew dark. Michael's heart grew heavy and fear swept over him.

Nevaeh pointed off to the distant southern horizon to a black speck in the sky. A swarm of bat demons and death birds were coming their way to tear them limb from limb.

"We don't have much time," Michael shouted. "Get ready for a fight!"

Four gigantic bat demons crashed through the glass windows of the factory. They must have stood at least nine feet tall, with broad, muscular shoulders, and were dressed in black leather garb. Their faces looked exactly like the faces of bats and they didn't wear any fly masks. Two of the demons were carrying bags of money with them. The third demon carried stacks of gold bricks in his hands. But the fourth bat demon had something strange in his hands. It looked like an egg or white stone. It was roughly four inches long, but he held it with both hands as if it was larger and much more precious than it appeared.

"White stone!" Noel cried as he jumped off the dirt bike.

Nevaeh yanked Noel back and said, "I love you, but you're an idiot. That isn't the white stone. It's just a holiday plastic egg."

All hell broke loose as the four bat demons pulled out automatic rifles and began to spray bullets all around, cackling with maniacal glee. Noel opened the top of the seat and pulled out guns, passing one to Nevaeh who spun and shot. She got off three shots before her brother turned around and hit the last one. One of the shots sliced through one of the bags of money, sending the paper bills fluttering all around. Nevaeh tilted her head and shot the plastic egg as it fell from the bat demon's hand. They waited, not even breathing, until the last of the bat demons hit the ground.

Noel shouted and pumped his fist while Nevaeh kept looking at the bodies for a few extra seconds. She put the gun down and said, "Good riddance."

Trip turned to the approaching cloud of enemies and took out the credit card holding the silver disk. She tossed it in the air and it started spinning. The deadly eye appeared in the middle of the silver as the flock of death drew closer and closer still.

Michael closed his eyes and summoned his warrior outfit while Trip did the same. Michael could see the flash of blue even through closed eyes and felt the power rush over him. As he blinked his eyes open, he felt something strange, something different. He slipped his hand into his pocket and pulled the plastic eye out. Why did this stay with him this time? Hadn't Trip been the one to carry it before? Had it chosen to switch to his possession?

The eye felt like it was humming, vibrating in his palm, so he tossed it into the air. The eye gleamed in the air and then split open, two gigantic white butterflies unfurling from the sides of the eyeball, growing until they were the size of a house with the tiny white start of the eye at the center.

The silver eye focused on one target and lasers flew from the center. The butterflies ran into the charge, shredding demons apart together before swooping towards their next target, their movement a beautiful dance of death.

Rain poured down from the skies and lightning flashed across clouds and into the ground below, a haunted reminder of the battle that waged on above them. Thunder shook the ground and the clouds split open, revealing, if only for a moment, the soft blue above. Before the hole closed, thousands of leaves fell out of the sky, followed by butterflies of all colors and sizes.

The Trues below watched in awe as the butterflies took control of the battle. Soon bodies began to rain against the ground in sickening thuds. One body missed the dirt bikes by a few feet, showing off the horrifying bite marks that covered the creature's wings and body. Michael's stomach turned to see all the deep, tearing marks where the butterflies had ripped the flesh from the monster's body. Even though they were evil, the carnage was gruesome to see. Nevaeh and Noel were giggling as they were shooting their guns at the flying dark creatures in the sky.

"Good shot!" Trip yelled over the thunder.

"This is so cool!" Noel shouted as he shot another death bird high in the sky.

It took less than fifteen minutes for the butterflies, lasers, and

Trues to wipe out the entire flock, the bodies of the monsters piling high around their small army of four.

"We won!" Noel cried, pumping his fist in the air with a whoop.

"We kicked some serious booty today," Nevaeh agreed, grinning ear to ear.

Michael couldn't help a small smile rise on his face. Nevaeh was a wonderful little girl. Michael couldn't help but love her because she was so brave and courageous. She was very special to him and maybe even for the world itself.

"What do we do now, Spirit Man?" Noel asked, standing beside his bike.

Michael scanned the scene for the plastic eye and found its pieces a few feet away. He picked it up, but it was clearly broken. He put one half to his eye and saw one set of butterflies pointing one way, but when he put the other half up to his eyes, it showed them staying put.

"These things are clearly broken. It's not supposed to be giving options," he said, holding the pieces in the palm of his hand. Maybe he had splintered their path with this choice, but he really didn't see any other choice he had.

Trip tapped her chin and looked around. "Well, what are the options that gross thing is giving you?"

Michael put the two halves back into his pocket and transformed back into his normal clothes. "We can keep going or we can stay here," he answered.

Nevaeh shook her head and said, "Let's keep going! This place is gonna start to be stinky if we stay for too long. We should keep going."

Noel nodded, hopping back on the dirt bike. "I agree. We need to keep moving to Horizon City. These beasts will hop up and march after us in their own time, anyway. Might as well give them a nice long journey to undertake before they get another crack at us."

Michael turned to Trip.

She shrugged.

He got on the bike and Trip got on behind him. There was something wonderful about the way her body pressed against his back, her arms around his waist. He nodded and said to the kids, "Sounds good to me. Lead the way."

Chapter 16

They were still following the tracks, the road red like a river of blood running through the cream sands of the desert. Desert brush stretched for miles in every direction as far as the eye could see, moving gently in the winds that swept the sands. The long empty roads were perfect for letting Michael's mind wander. Horizon City. How far was it? Who was the Sun King, really? The image of Atlas plucking out his eye flickered across his mind. How in the world did he grow a new eyeball that fast? And what were they going to do now that the one he gave them was broken?

So many images. So many colors. So many things seen and unseen.

Over the weeks of their travel through the desert, Noel told Michael and Trip many interesting and controversial things about the Sun King and his wife that he and Nevaeh had learned. It was clear enough that it was true the Sun King was old and dying, and that his wife died as well. But the manner of her death seemed shrouded in mystery. Did she really die of natural causes or was she murdered by someone in the court? There were many different characters milling about the castle, with different levels of suspicion. Maids who called in sick the day during the death. A cook that couldn't remember what she made for dinner. A powerful magician who was knowledgeable about plants. It could have been any of them really, though the king himself wasn't completely above suspicion. Nevaeh would clam up whenever the topic was mentioned, almost disappearing into herself with a distant, unreadable look on her face, so Michael did his best to ask Noel questions when she wasn't especially near.

It was clear the young boy thought the magician did it. His name was J.C. Blackstone, and he liked power and attention, no matter what kind. He did magic tricks in front of the city's people every afternoon, gleefully absorbing the praise and cheers of the crowd. The people as well as the king and queen seemed very fond of him. But the queen grew sick so he made her a special tea with honey. He brought it to her in her chambers and left without a word. The queen sipped on the hot tea and the next piece of information was the maid finding her dead the next morning.

"Or that's how the story goes," Noel said as he bit into some bread. "In reality, it was a bit different. J.C. Blackstone stayed with the queen that night as he often did, telling tales about life beyond the desert and sea. He was there as she died, but he wasn't the only one. Guess who was hiding in the closet and witnessed the murder of the queen? Nevaeh."

"Why was she hiding?" Michael asked quietly.

Noel seemed proud to reveal this information all of a sudden; Michael thought that this might explain why Nevaeh clammed up every time the subject arose in conversation on their travels.

Noel shrugged. "The Moon Queen and Sun King loved us. They treated us like their own kids and let us stay in the castle while we waited for Trip to find us. We often played hide and seek in the giant castle, but Nevaeh also got permission to be in the queen's quarters because she loved the queen's dresses. But J.C. Blackstone found out she was there when she tried to attack him. He stole her knee-caps and was about to do worse. I managed to find her right in time and get us away, but before I knew it, the castle guards were looking for us. J.C. claimed that Nevaeh was the last one who saw the queen alive and had probable cause."

Tears flowed down the boy's cheeks and Michael was stunned. "And you want to go back even if they suspect you both?"

"The king is in trouble. We want him to know the truth, but it's likely that J.C. already is preparing for that. But we have to help. The Sun King and Moon Queen were so kind to us."

Michael knelt down next to the boy and put a hand on his shoulder. "I promise that we will do all we can to help."

Noel smiled but also warned him that the magician was tricky.

What was Michael going to do when they got to Horizon City? He had to help the sun not die, but he also had to protect the kids.

The sun sank lower in the sky like a deflating balloon the closer they got as the group wound down the red road. They passed many fascinating sights, like the Devil's Backbone, a park full of huge rocks that formed any shape Michael could think of. Swans, camels, dogs, cats, turtles, anything. They passed a still pond that killed anything that touched it. If Trip hadn't noticed the carcasses of rotting animals, the shreds of dead plants, just beneath the surface of the water, they might have been tricked by the crystal blue inviting waters.

But they were getting close. Michael could feel it in his bones. The red road shifted into a wide paved road that looked like a superhighway. The new road stretched for miles and miles as far as his eye could see. If the position of the sun was at all correct, the road was heading due west. The two dirt bikes moved along at a steady pace. Michael noticed some unusual words on the side of the road, painted in a hundred colors. "The Path of the Sun God" was repeated over and over again as they drove, an obsessive repetition of the words until they seemed to lose all meaning. A huge highway sign was above them on the road. The green sign with white trim read, "Horizon City, 2DW."

The caravan pulled up right underneath the highway sign, happy for a brief moment where the sun wasn't scorching their skin.

"How far is 2DW?" Noel asked.

"I don't even know what 2DW means!" Michael laughed.

Nevaeh rolled her eyes and said, "2DW just means that we are getting closer. We are only a few worlds away from our destination."

"Great!" Michael said, then added after a moment, "So, how far is that?" He wanted to ask if there was a conversion rate between miles and worlds, but he had a feeling Trip would roll her eyes at him. Plus, it wasn't exactly like the dream worlds to hold to specific measurements like that.

"Ugh. Does Horizon City even exist?" Trip asked. "We are in an awful mess. We don't even know where we are going or if this place

exists." She looked around the desert, the lack of civilization anywhere around them.

Noel glared at Trip and said, "We were there before. We just didn't
use a road to get there or to leave, so it's a bit hard to tell how to get
there using one."

Michael turned to the boy. "What do you mean, you didn't use a
road?" he asked.

Noel turned red. Nevaeh put a hand on her brother's shoulder and
said, "We used the blue doors. The door would lead us directly into
the queen's royal closet and we explored the rest of the castle from
there. We never actually went outside the castle itself while there,
but we did see out the windows and heard the people talking about
the city." She sighed. "So, in those terms, we can't actually vouch
for the fact that the city is approachable in this way. I'm sorry we
weren't completely honest before." She looked to Noel with concern on her face. "We—we weren't sure how to tell you about our
experience, and how it would affect our journey. So we didn't tell
you and just acted like we knew the road would get us there for sure.
I'm sorry."

She sounded so pitiful that Michael couldn't feel that much anger,
though this revelation certainly changed things.

Michael rubbed between his eyes and said, "Well, at least you're
telling the truth now. That's what matters."

Trip sighed and said, "You're right. I'm sorry for doubting you,
Nevaeh. But we are still at the problem of not knowing exactly how
to get to the city."

Nevaeh's eyes lit up and she said, "I might be able to find the door
again if we get in the city next to it."

Trip nodded, steel coming back to her features. "That's the spirit!
We can do this."

They climbed back on their bikes and drove off. A white dove appeared in the sky and followed them, curious to see where they
would go. They drove for days, weeks, and perhaps even months
while heading west. They got lost and yet they pushed on toward
Horizon City. The caravan rolled on and on. Another week or two

　　　　　　　　　　　DREAM OF THE SPIRIT MAN

passed until they finally saw something in the far distance. Still the white dove sailed high above them as they made their way across the desert wastelands of nowhere.

Chapter 11

Michael and the band of Trues traveled for the next three months across the wastelands. They followed the superhighway to nowhere, the sun sinking further in the sky the closer they got. Time wasn't marked by day or night, but by the slow crawl of the sun as it inched closer to the horizon with each day of travel. Michael grew used to falling asleep with a cover over his eyes to keep out the sunlight, since there was no night to wait for.

There was no need for a map as the road always headed due west. The terrain didn't shift or change much, dust and desert as far as they eye could see, straight flat swaths of brown that clung to everything. The kids' shining dirt bike turned dull and brown and slowly the color felt like it was sinking into them, clouding their very lungs. Then one day the scenery completely changed. In the far distance, a blood red mountain range grew in the western sky. The shadow passed over them and darkness cloaked the group. The highway lost a lane on one side and then the other, until just one dirt bike could go in front of the other. The road twisted up the mountain, surrounded by dead trees. Hawks perched on the top of the dead branches but there were no death birds in sight.

They were high up in the mountains when dark black clouds rolled across the sky, blocking out the sun. Michael couldn't help but be grateful for the merciful break from the sun, even as thunder rumbled in the deep dark of the clouds. Lightning cackled and shot across the angry sky as rain poured down. A faint red tint tinged the clouds and the rain began to belch forth onto the land below. An acid smell began to fill the air.

"Bleeding clouds," Michael whispered. "This can't be good."

"Where are we now, Nevaeh?" Noel asked, nervous.

"I'm not entirely sure," Nevaeh whispered back. "But I do think this is dangerous."

Trip cursed under her breath. "That doesn't sound good at all. What do we do? Should we keep pushing forward or wait for the rain to stop?"

Michael shook his head and said, "I don't think this rain is going to stop, not until we pass this mountain. Keep an eye out and shoot anything that's threatening."

The kids nodded, and Nevaeh pulled her gun out on her lap, her eye sharp for what was ahead.

The hawks turned toward them as they sped up the road but did not make a single noise. They just sat there, perched on the dead branches of long dead trees.

The pulled around a corner and Michael came to a jarring stop. Up ahead, standing in the middle of the road, was a small group of zombies. They were an ugly group of bandits that carried all kinds of swords, clubs, and spears. Most of the zombies were slack jawed, missing a piece here or there, a gaping piece of their brains, a chunk of their guts. The leader had zebra stripes painted across his ugly face and blood was dripping out of the corner of his mouth.

Noel came to a halt right behind Michael, a bit too close for comfort.

The leader held up a shattered spear, its pieces held together with string and tar. "Don't come closer, Spirit Man. We will kill you."

The other zombies grunted their agreement. "There is no white stone that can save your world from the destruction it has been seeking," the leader of the zombies continued. He was surprisingly articulate for what Michael would have expected of a zombie. The rest may not have that level of intelligence, though; perhaps the ability to form sentences like this was why this one was the leader, as the other zombies seemed to be groaning unintelligibly behind him.

Michael held his head high and said to the zombie leader, "We need to pass. Clear the way or we will clear through you."

The leader laughed and lightning cut across the sky, illuminating twenty bat demons looking on, hanging from the mountain sides.

He jabbed his spear forward and the zombies and demons charged forward.

Michael lifted his feet from the ground and shifted into first, then second, gunning toward the zombies on the ground. Trip pulled out two handguns and started firing, two head shots for each zombie she saw, carving a small path for Michael to navigate. "Noel, Nevaeh, get somewhere safe!" she cried out over the thunder as she fired into the swarm. The shots from her gun blended in with the thunder from the clouds until Michael wasn't sure what was her shooting and what was the thunder clapping above.

The twins shared a meaningful glance and Nevaeh picked up the two handguns in her lap and started shooting while Noel drove, following the path Michael and Trip mowed clear ahead of them.

One of Nevaeh's guns jammed, and she tossed it at the face of a bat demon getting a bit too close. She closed her eyes and reached out with her left hand to touch her brother's side. A soft blue glow covered her, and her eyes sprung open, bright blue. She grinned, and her feet flew out of the side cart and started kicking demons that were getting a bit too close. She used her free hand to aim her handgun at others, spotting a path. "Spirit Man, there is a broken bridge! If you can jump it, we'll be safe."

Michael nodded confirmation that he'd heard her and spun the dirt bike around, gunning for the broken path while Trip kept up the heavy fire at the demons and zombies everywhere around them. The front tire hit the incline perfectly and the bike soared over the chasm, Trip swiveling around in her seat to shoot a zombie that was reaching for her ankle. The bike hit the ground on the other side and Michael pulled a hard stop, jumping off to take out some of the last bat demons.

On the other side of the bridge, Noel turned to aim his bike at the chasm and took a deep breath. Nevaeh squeezed his side and said, "You can do this."

Noel nodded and took off toward the gap. Time seemed to slow down as something caught in the back wheel just as it was leaving the ground. The kids tilted forward, thrown from the bike. Michael and Trip screamed on the other side of the chasm, lunging for the falling twins. Michael caught Nevaeh's hands in time as Noel slipped further. Trip twisted her hands off and they flew after the boy, catching him but just slowing him down. Noel cried out, "Trip!" Her hands gripped his shirt, desperately trying to reverse his descent. Sweat broke out on Trip's forehead and she gritted her teeth, digging her heels down into the sand and leaning the rest of her body back.

Michael pulled Nevaeh out of the chasm. Trip leaned back, and the boy was flying up through the air, colliding into her. She held onto him tightly as they both broke down into tears, clinging to each other. Michael stood nearby, holding onto Nevaeh, clearly shaking when Trip pulled him down into the group hug. The four clung to each other as the rain poured down, washing their panic and fear and the gore of their battle into the earth.

Finally, Trip was the first to let go and stand back up, screaming as she fired into what remained of the zombies across the cavern, crowded around the ramp they'd used to launch across the chasm. She fired as they fell and fired until her guns could fire no more. Michael got up, setting Nevaeh by her brother and rested a hand on Trip's shoulder. The guns stopped firing and her arms dropped as she turned, burying her face into his chest as she sobbed. "Why do we have to go through this? Why does this keep happening? Why can't ...why can't they just be kids?"

Michael held her tight, unable to say anything. It wasn't fair that they had to keep going through this. That they had to face death on a daily basis. It wasn't fair. For the kids or for Trip. They seemed so cheerful for the most part, but Michael realized that they had to be. If they didn't force themselves to laugh and smile in this place, then they would never have the chance to. The only thing he could think, the only thing he could say, was, "I'm sorry." It wasn't enough for the gulf of pain and suffering that surrounded them, but it was all he had to offer.

The rain slowed down before Trip pulled away, her shoulders still trembling before she turned to the kids. Forced laughter came from Nevaeh, trying to brush everything off. Michael turned and watched the scene behind them. The hawks shifted and took to the air, showing jagged beaks as they descended on the corpses they left behind. It made sense. After all, they were hungry and ready to eat. The vicious beaks tore into the zombies' flesh and giant jagged mouths opened on the hawks' stomachs, devouring what their claws ripped apart.

When Michael could stomach no more of this sight, he turned around, seeing Nevaeh bury her face into Trip's shoulder, sobbing. Michael was at a loss for words. How was he supposed to help this little girl from this strange world they were lost in? Nothing made sense anymore. So much pain with no relief in sight.

Chapter 18

As a group, they decided there was no use in continuing on in the state they were in. Better to make camp for the night and recover from the battle and the scare of jumping the chasm. Trip and the twins got camp ready and Michael was glad that they moved some of the provisions over to their bike. But what were they going to do now? He offered to take first watch and watched as Trip fell asleep with one of the twins in each arm. In sleep, all three of them looked so alike it was impossible not to see that they were family.

Michael decided to do what he could while the rest slept, seeing what they did have left. They had two sleeping bags, some assorted food cans, two chairs. They would survive but would lose a lot of the lead that they had managed to gain on Raven Bones and his forces. But it couldn't be helped if they only had one dirt bike. The biggest question now was what they could do for Nevaeh. She didn't exactly have knees to walk through the desert on her own. Michael could carry her while Trip and Noel took the bike. But would she be fine with that? She was closer to Trip, but he didn't like the thought of her walking all that way when she didn't have to. And this was no time for pride or ego.

Trip woke up for her shift and Michael jerked his head away from their little camp. She looked confused but nodded, following him a bit out of the way. Michael ran a hand through his hair and said, "I've been thinking since everyone else went to sleep. What are we going to do? Trip, we need to have some kind of plan, and I'm not sure right now what that is."

She looked at him like he lost his mind. "We've been traveling for at least half a year. Don't tell me you forgot why."

He struggled not to roll his eyes as he said, "No, about the one bike, about Nevaeh."

Trip crossed her arms over her chest and said, "Don't worry. We will figure something out. We always do. Besides, the bikes are Noel's idea so maybe he can pull something off. Don't you trust us? We've had each other's lives in our hands all this way. If you can just trust us, I'm sure we'll be fine like we always have been."

She walked back but turned when she realized he wasn't following her. "You do trust us, right? Michael?"

She tilted her head at him, and he took a moment to figure out how to phrase his answer. He didn't want to hurt her, but it was important that he communicate honestly with her.

"It's not that I don't trust you. If anything, I have no choice but to trust you. You three know this world better than I ever could. But I don't want to lose you three, any of you. I keep getting flashes of nightmares or memories, where you are all shot and there was nothing I could do. And the children were almost lost again today. I can't lose you. Not again."

Her hand was on his cheek, wiping off a tear he didn't realize had fallen. "I can't guarantee we won't die again. There is a good chance it will happen, actually. But we have to keep going. You have to trust us, not only to take care of ourselves in battle but that if we do die, we will try our best to find each other." She shrugged, intentionally making light of the situation. "Trust is all I have to reassure me if you die again, too. I think trust might be all we have, Michael."

He leaned into her hand, holding it to his face before pulling it away to intertwine their fingers. He brought her fingers to his lips and took her hand in both of his. "I trust you, Trip. I trust you with my life, and I'll trust you with it over and over again. It's that I don't trust myself. What if I forget again? What if you lose something else because I...?" He couldn't say it out loud: *because I forget you ever existed.*

His hands explored over her fingers, brushing down her wrists where it could disconnect, feeling the faint raised line where the flesh could be screwed off. He noticed her shiver as she put her other hand up to stop his gentle exploration. "Can't lose me that easily," she murmured. "Not the first time, not the second or the thousandth

                              DREAM OF THE SPIRIT MAN

or the millionth. Nothing this world throws at me will ever stop me from searching you out and doing what I can to help you remember. We don't know what will happen. We can't control the future. We can just prepare and do our best. It's all we can really do."

She smiled and intertwined their fingers once again. "Come on. You should get some rest. We're close but we got a ways to go still."

Michael nodded and let her lead him back to the small camp where he fell into a dreamless sleep. He wanted to be more comforted by her words, but a part of him couldn't forget the way she'd spoken in Satan's Pass about his memory, how being forgotten had hurt her. He couldn't deny that he had, and it frightened him to think that his own mind could withhold his memories from him so completely, even with someone as important to him as Trip and the kids.

He woke up to the smell of bacon and beans and soft whispers over the fire. Trip smiled softly when he walked over and said, "What's the plan for today?"

She squeezed Michael's hand, letting it drop after a moment. He smiled at her.

Nevaeh was the one who answered Michael's question. "Trip promised to teach me a bit about how to use my legs and stuff while Noel tries to figure out how to make something that can hold all of us. He might need your help getting stuff from the pile of corpses across the gorge."

Noel crossed his arms and said, "Hey, there is a chance we have enough materials as it is."

Nevaeh rolled her eyes and said, "Oh really? What are you gonna turn into parts? The two chairs we have? Or the pan? You know, the stuff we still need."

Noel let out a long dramatic sigh and said, "Extra parts could be helpful. What I'm gonna try to make will definitely be bare bones as it is. There should be some way to cross back over and grab some metal parts. Guns, pitchforks, swords, anything as long as it's metal. Can you do that?"

Michael nodded and started searching out the area. It didn't look like there was an easy way to get across, especially now that Noel had mostly dismantled the one dirt bike they had. Michael turned to the giant dead trees and flashed into his warrior outfit. The eyeballs floated above his shoulders and he focused on the base of one of the trees, trying to aim it such a way that it would fall across the gap. The lasers went off with a blast and the tree cracked, falling across the way with a thundering crash as it hit the other side. Michael jumped up on the makeshift bridge, carefully nudging the trunk to see if it would fall apart as he made it across.

It was a good thing that Noel needed metal and not any parts of the zombies as the bodies were already reduced to bones. The hawks had worked fast through the night, and he could feel their gaze from the treetops. They wanted him to die, too, for their hunger, and if he took too long, they would do their best to hurry the process.

Michael kept the warrior outfit on, ready to attack any of the birds that decided they couldn't wait for his death by natural means. He gathered all he could in his arms and made it back over, making several trips, but none of the birds attacked.

When he got back, Noel had completely dismantled the bike and placed all the pieces in the magically spacious seat. He grabbed the piles of metal Michael brought over and dropped them into the seat.

"How does this work?" Michael asked.

Noel shrugged and said, "Conservation of matter. You need stuff in order to make other stuff. Things can't just come from nothing. I'm not as powerful as Trip yet, so I need a space where I can put things and I have to physically pull them apart and put them together. 'Course I can use stuff more than once though."

Trip walked over and said, "Hey, don't go spilling my secrets. And I can totally use stuff more than once. It's just that it's hard to remember exactly how much I got. Can't overestimate or the thing I make will fall apart or have holes. And it takes a while for things to pop in and out of existence."

Michael turned to her, wide eyed. "You mean you collected enough metal for a tank?"

"About that much, yeah. I was saving up for a while, but I figured it would be worth it."

Nevaeh laughed. "Oh please. You are totally showing off for your love," she sang.

Trip glared at the younger girl who just laughed all the harder. A small smile passed over her lips and she shrugged. "Okay, part of it may have been showing off. Are you about done with your warmups, Nevaeh? I'd love to see what you can do."

Noel nudged Michael, handing him pieces and parts, and they started working together to build Noel's latest vision.

Trip twisted off her hands and they clasped together in front of her. "Okay, so what are your limits using your limbs?"

Nevaeh's feet floated a few feet above ground. She started doing a little jig. "They can do whatever I feel they should."

Trip shook her head. "No, they can only do about however much you could do if you were still attached to them. Independently, of course. Your feet don't have to stay within a certain range of each other. And within one hundred feet of you."

Nevaeh groaned and looked up in the sky, her feet swinging. "I know all this. Why do you continue to harp on it?"

"Because you seem to be forgetting things. If you know so much, how well do you control the pieces when you can't see them? What happens if they get captured? What happens if you die before you get them back? I haven't been going over these things because I thought you decided it wasn't worth the risk using them when you don't have your knees anymore."

"Trip, I had to use my legs yesterday. We were getting overwhelmed and we needed—"

Trip put up her hand. "I know. I'm not saying you did the wrong thing. I just want to make sure you know the potential consequences and guidelines. If you die before you get your knees back, you won't only lose your knees but your calves and feet as well. Even if you still have them with you."

Nevaeh rolled her eyes. "How would you know? There isn't anyone else who can do this but us."

"I know because of my brother." Trip's words were quiet, but so unexpected that everyone else fell silent and looked to her to hear them.

Nevaeh's mouth snapped shut and her legs stopped swinging. Her voice was quiet and soft when it came out. "You had a brother?"

Trip nodded, focusing on weaving her hands around, watching as they screwed themselves back on her wrists. "Everyone born here has a twin. And it wasn't just us and you two goofballs that were born here. There are rumors of another pair. But that might be a story for another day. Yes, I had a brother. His name was Trap."

Michael shifted slightly so he could watch the conversation better. Trip had a brother? Where was he now? What happened? How was there still so much that he didn't know about her and her past?

Trip ground her teeth together and said, "I wouldn't be sharing this unless I thought it would help. You have to know the horror of what can happen."

She closed her eyes and clasped her hands together. "He was the most reckless person I knew. This happened during the first passage, before the demons attacked. Before people started dying because of the war. Before we knew what it did to people. And Trap would do stupid things all the time, just because he could. He thought we were invincible. Then one time, he died and he found out he could remove his arms after that. He thought it was the coolest thing ever. He would practice sword fights, ask someone to shoot him, and pull stupid stunts like walking over a fifty-foot cavern blindfolded, figuring death couldn't hurt him the same way it hurt the rest of the Trues. I was doing research on the Death Birds and Bat Demons at the time. I didn't realize how bad it had gotten until he showed up one day and could remove parts at every joint. It started when he lost the middle joint off his left pinky finger."

She opened her eyes and looked at her own hand. "Did you know that with each death, the connection becomes a little bit easier to remove? I have to screw my hands off my wrists manually, but his just floated off when he wanted. He had to focus twenty-four seven to keep all his parts. I found him sobbing in my office when he found out his parts were gone forever if he lost them now. He got desperate. We tried a few things, from putting his pieces in a chest, just the tip of his pinky toe, just to see if they would keep. He came back the next freaking day and we found out it had disintegrated. Of course that's around the time the battle started breaking off. We didn't understand what was happening, why people suddenly wore white and tried to destroy everyone around them."

She took a deep breath and the air shuddered as it left her lungs. "He was recruited. He died the most by accident and nothing bad seemed to happen to him. Why wouldn't he be fine going into battle? We would often go into battle together. Do you know why, Nevaeh?"

Nevaeh looked at the ground and said, "'Cause we are more powerful when we are close to each other." Michael looked at her curiously. He hadn't realized that Noel and Nevaeh had that power before... Did that mean he'd only met Trip at less power than she was capable of? That was a frightening thought. She was formidable enough as it was.

Trip nodded and said, "It up to doubles our range and strength when we are close, especially if we are touching. But in one battle, I didn't die. I broke my leg. One officer suggested to just put a bullet between my eyes. Death 'fixes' things like that, after all. But my brother refused to let them. He said he would be fine. But then he didn't come back."

Tears dripped down her face and Nevaeh wobbled over, wrapping her arms around Trip. Trip leaned into her and said, "Apparently the other side gained its first general. Its second would of course be the asshole who offered to shoot me, but that's a different story. Random attacks grew coordinated. It took six months for me to gather the time and people to look for him. They experimented on him. When I found him, he was just a head and a body separated from me by glass and magic."

Trip stepped back, holding Nevaeh at arm's length. "I don't want what happened to him to happen to anyone else. I'm not telling you to scare you but to tell you what is all too likely to happen. You have to watch over your parts. You have to be careful. Please."

Nevaeh looked down at the ground. "I will try to keep a better eye, but I don't regret doing what I had to when I lost my knees. I had to do something."

Trip hugged her and said, "Things happen. It's okay. As long as you come out the other side, it will end up being okay. Now let's get back to training."

Nevaeh nodded and was more serious now as Trip took her through some training exercises, working to master her control over her flying limbs.

In a few hours, Michael and Noel were done putting the pieces together, creating a small golf cart that could hold four people along with two more chairs.

That night, after the twins fell asleep, Michael turned to Trip. She shook her head and said, "I don't want to talk about it, Michael. I can already tell you have questions and I just can't right now. Okay?"

Michael nodded and said, "That's more than fair. I just wanted you to know, if you needed to tell anyone, I'd be willing to listen."

She shook her head, her hand on his shoulder. "Thank you. But I'm not ready to talk about that yet. Please don't push it."

Michael nodded and said, "Okay." She leaned her head on his shoulder and they looked into the fire in quiet thought as the night passed.

Chapter 19

The next day, they gathered all their supplies and put it in the space under the seat and took off on the road once again. Noel and Nevaeh were in the front, while Michael and Trip got the back. They followed the superhighway until it abruptly narrowed and ended. The road shifted into a wide dirt road that led to a small town named Bog. The cart rolled to a halt near the first broken-down wooden buildings. Most of the signs in town were faded. There was no one on the streets but one small raccoon with gold rings around its eyes scampering around the corner.

Michael got out of the cart and shouted out, "Anyone here?"

A furry head popped out of the saloon and scampered into the street, ready to flee at any moment. He was dressed in jean overalls and gold rimmed eyes. Other animals peaked out, sneaking closer. The raccoon's nose twitched as he got closer and said in a small, squeaky voice, "Friend or foe?"

"Friend as long as you are one," Michael answered the odd little creature.

The raccoon tilted his head and sniffed the air before nodding. "Fair enough. Name's Miles. Welcome to Bog."

Trip jumped out of the golf cart and Noel waved and said, "So what's in this little town?"

Miles said, "Well, there's the Barber shop, but I don't think that would be much interest to y'all. Bob's a blacksmith if you need any tools and such. But really the only thing in this little town is the Bog Saloon. Great food and cheap booze, what more can you need?"

Michael turned to Trip, who said, "Thanks for the recommendations but we really can't linger here long enough to take in all the sights. We've got a lot of stuff to do, and a long journey still to go."

Nevaeh pouted and said, "I want to eat something besides canned food and burritos."

Noel nodded and added, "I want to drink!"

Michael turned to the boy with a disapproving look but shrugged. "Food would be good." He looked to Trip. "Just a short stop, maybe? Lunch? Then we'll head out right after."

Trip sighed, clearly still not preferring to stop, but eventually nodded and gave in. The kids gave a little cheer.

Miles smiled and walked towards the Saloon. "Sure! We got lots of grub that isn't grubs. Come on and stay a while! We got fried chicken, wings, biscuits and gravy and lots of beer to boot."

Michael shrugged and they all followed the raccoon to the Saloon. That afternoon, and well into the evening, Michael and the band of Trues ate and drank as much as they could. Michael had a talk with the Moose behind the bar not to serve anything alcoholic to the twins, but Noel was still swaying by the end. Everyone ate everything in sight, from pizza, chicken, and fries, to biscuits and gravy and waffles. By this time, Nevaeh was the only one in the bar that still acted sober and sane. The trues linked arms with the animals and danced all through the night, singing the songs they knew and even some that they didn't.

The clocks chimed at midnight when a group of dark Saviors came riding into town on horses that were black as night. They held guns high over their head, shooting a volley into the air. The party inside froze and the head Savior cried out, "Bring out the Spirit Man and we won't burn the whole town down with you inside it."

The animals all gathered weapons, ready to defend their little town, but kept a close eye on the strangers that brought the danger to them. Noel and Nevaeh brought out their guns while Trip looked ready to defend them at any given moment. Michael staggered to the door, barely able to keep on his feet while summoning his own weaponry. Trip shouted, "Michael, don't!" Her voice was wobbly with the booze, but the fear was clear in her tone.

The animals all turned to each other and nodded, coming to the consensus that they were going to help in whatever way they could.

Michael smiled up at Trip, though sadness tinted the corners.

"Trip, these people are in danger 'cuz I'm here right now. I can't just sit back and let them fight for me. I got to help in any way I can."

Trip glared at him, clearly fighting the decision before nodding. "You better come back to me, Spirit Man. I won't forgive you if you don't."

Michael smiled and squeezed her hand before heading out the door, "Keep Noel and Nevaeh safe. I'll be back."

The leader of the Saviors sauntered over to the Saloon and said, "Well look what we have here. The brave unkillable Spirit Man looks a bit vulnerable. This may be a lot easier than we had hoped." He turned to his men and shouted, "Kill the Spirit Man and any who fight at his side!"

The battle was quick but fierce. The saviors aimed their muskets at Michael and the animals but were being picked off faster and faster. They managed a few return shots, knocking the Saviors off their horses but all too soon Michael was the only one left on his side while the enemy forces were still strong on the other side. Michael staggered as a shot blasted into his left shoulder. The leader called off the shooting with a wave of his hand and walked toward Michael, blood pouring from wounds from his arms and legs, ones that barely brushed him, but it built up. Michael wobbled, and the leader brought out his gun and put it right in the center of Michael's chest. With a defining blast, Michael crumpled to the ground and the leader called out, "Let it be known that it was Blade Duvall who finally killed the Spirit Man!"

Trip howled and lunged for the door, only for a bear with gold rimmed eyes to hold her back as Nevaeh and Noel clung to each other in shock. Miles ran out the door glaring up at Blade Duvall. "You did what you came to do. Leave now."

Duvall looked the tiny raccoon in the eyes and kicked Michael in the side and aimed his gun at Michael again, firing once more for a point before saying, "You do not get to tell me what to do. Soon, Miles, you will find out there is no other way but the truth and you will have to follow me."

Duvall looked down at the body and spat on the ground, "But for now, I'll let the fruitlessness of fighting us settle in. Saviors! Head out."

Duvall kicked Michael's body out of the way and walked out of town.

Trip and the twins didn't move as the bear finally released her and the other animals started grabbing the bodies of their friends and repairing what they could. They were shaking, trying to figure out why the world they lived was such that they lived, and Michael died. Trip ran to the body, and whispered, "Michael, you promised."

She fell down to her knees and held on to him tight. Noel carried his sister over and Nevaeh rolled her eyes. "No point in that. He'll vanish and appear again like he always does."

Trip turned to the twins, looking at them without seeing them. "But what will it cost? He made me a promise. Will he keep it?"

Noel put his sister down on the steps and hugged Trip tightly. "You know we can't choose the cost. If he doesn't remember, he doesn't remember. But we have to keep fighting. It's what he would have wanted."

They stared at the body, waiting for it to vanish, to move, to do anything, but it stayed put. When the clock chimed eight, Trip was pacing by his body and said, "Why hasn't something happened yet? I always disappear when I die, right?"

Noel nodded. "Yeah, if you don't come back right then. But whatever happens always happens before sunrise."

Nevaeh looked panicked. "There is no sunrise or sunset in this realm. What if he can't come back? Besides, Michael isn't originally a part of this world. What if the rules don't work the same for him?"

Trip held the body's hand and shook her head, not moving at all. "He has to come back. He promised. He promised."

Nevaeh put her hand on Trip's shoulder and said, "He would if he could."

Noel looked at the body and said, "What if he is trying to keep that promise right now?"

Nevaeh rolled her eyes. "What are you talking about?"

"Well, what if he is trying to return to his body but is stuck? What if he is trying to avoid the consequence and just come back to this body without it healing at all? What if he is stuck there, in a body that can't move?"

Trip shook her head. "Why would the forces of life and death be so cruel?"

A warm breeze swept over the desert, picking up dust and tumbleweeds.

Miles came out the door, the light shining from the gold rings around his eyes as he saw the trues surrounding Michael. "Life and death have a strange relationship in Bog. But there is a way to get your friend back. Take him to the Field of Dreams and hope that the spirits will help. But know this, if you choose to do so, they will ask something from you as well."

Trip nodded and, with the help of the animals, put Michael's body in the golf cart. Miles looked over at his fallen comrades and the death that sank into the very ground. "I can lead you there, but I can only go so far. Please understand, the spirits ask what they think is needed. If it is too much, you can deny them."

The twins nodded but Trip didn't. "Michael is important to me and this realm. Whatever the spirits ask, it can't be too much."

Miles shrugged and said, "Sometimes we cannot know the cost of a thing until after it has already been paid, and by then it's too late to say it's too much. Just be careful. Don't give more than you can."

Miles gave out directions for Noel. "I'd go with you if I could, but one of the trades I made asked for me to never come back. Please work to bring the night again."

The drive was quiet, though Nevaeh tried to fill the air with sound. There was a mirth missing, a doubt creeping on the edge of the trues' minds. Noel followed the instructions past Bog, past a dry lakebed, past the dirt into a forest as the trees grew taller and taller. He drove until the road ran out and there was nothing else around. Trip pulled Michael out of the golf cart and carried him to the center of the clearing, telling the twins to stay back.

She put the body in the center of the field and sat down beside him and waited. She waited in silence as the breeze brushed over the grass below, each moment agonizing. The tall grasses beyond the clearing began to sway back and forth as a strong wind blew down the middle of it. The wind swirled, full of soft red light that solidified as the sound of a horn sounded in the distance. A red stag stepped out of the light, noble and crowned with golden antlers as a cape of moss flowed from his back. He looked down at Michael and looked into Trip's eyes.

A deep voice echoed in her head and she knew that she was the only one who could hear it.

"Welcome, child, what do you come to ask?"

The voice sounded like the wind through the trees, like water lapping at the shore of a lake. She could understand it perfectly, but as soon as the voice finished speaking, she forgot what it sounded like.

Trip looked down at Michael's body and said, "Can you bring him back?"

The stag hovered over Michael and sniffed the air. "He is with you now."

Trip shook her head and said, "He's dead, can you bring him to life again?"

The stag snorted. "You humans have an odd sense of life and death. He has not passed on yet."

Trip squeezed Michael's hand and said, "What should I do?"

"Now that is a question I can help with. You can kill him yourself and the gods will extract a consequence. Or I could heal him enough for him to wake up. But I, too, have a price."

Trip turned to the twins sitting in the golf cart and noticed that they hadn't moved since the stag appeared. The red stag shook his head and said, "This is your decision and yours alone to make. I would make it quickly. I do not know how much longer this Michael of yours will stay. Now is not the time to linger in indecision."

Trip was confident as she looked at the red stag and said, "Heal him please. I'll do whatever you need. I just need him here with me."

The stag nodded and leaned down over Michael. He was inches away when he opened his mouth and began to breathe tiny bubbles out of his mouth. There were thousands of tiny bubbles in all kinds of colors. They drifted slowly down, popping as they touched Michael's body, leaving a gleaming sheen of rainbow over his skin for a second before the substance was absorbed into the skin. Where the bubbles popped, the wounds healed a bit more and a bit more until they were almost gone.

The stag breathed bubbles until Michael gasped for breath and started coughing. Then the red stag lifted its massive head and stared at Trip.

Tears were flowing out of Trip's eyes as she clung to Michael. "Thank you."

The stag blinked and said, "Now for your side. I want you to kill the Sun King."

Chapter 20

Trip turned to the stag and said, "What?"

"I want you to kill the Sun King. You will have two weeks, at which point if it has not been done, I will take my aid away, as well as an additional cost for my wasted time and magic. It is fair, is it not? I can't do my part and have you neglect yours."

The stag pulled its great head up to its full height and Trip realized exactly how inhuman it really was.

Her gut dropped.

"Why do you want the Sun King to die?" Trip demanded.

The red stag snorted and said, "He insulted me. There is nothing else you need to know."

With that, the red stag turned and vanished as he walked away, fading into the air as if he had never existed at all.

Michael convulsed on the ground, and Trip turned to him. The twins shouted out and Noel ran forward. "What did you do, Trip? He's coming back!"

Trip was shaking as she looked up at the twins. She couldn't tell them. She couldn't tell any of them. The twins wanted to save the Sun King. She couldn't take an innocent life, could she?

But the look Michael gave her as he woke up, full of love and admiration, such joy to just see her face, broke her willpower. She couldn't lose him. She had to do as the red stag asked. Any price was worth it to see Michael looking up at her again.

Michael reached up, just barely brushing her face with his fingers, and said, "I was so scared, Trip. I thought I would forget you again."

She gave a laugh that broke in pieces with sobs in between. She wrapped his hand with hers as tears dripped down her face. "I thought I lost you."

Nevaeh threw her arms around Michael and cried, "You're alive!

We thought you would be gone forever."

"Can't lose me that easily," Michael whispered as he let out a hollow laugh.

Noel clung to Michael and started sobbing, just holding on.

Michael pulled back from the group and said, "What happened back there? Are the animals okay?"

Noel's head dropped as he said, "Several died. Miles is okay, and the bear helped keep us safe. I should have fought next to you. I'm sorry."

Michael groaned as he sat up a bit more, reaching toward Noel. "Don't you dare blame yourself for that. You did what you had to. They were only after me. I would have rather died one thousand times over again than for any of you to be hurt because of me. Speaking of that, Trip, I can't figure out what happened because I died. I remember everything I knew before. My hands are still attached. Does the price of death and rebirth just take a while to kick in?"

Trip shook her head and Nevaeh said quickly, "Trip traded something with the red stag, so you won't have to deal with the consequence of death this time."

Michael jerked back in shock as Trip helped him to his feet, almost falling back onto the ground. "I would have come back sometime anyway. Why did you go bartering for me?" Michael demanded.

She couldn't look in his eyes and Noel started talking, "Apparently, people don't come back in this area. You need the sunset and sunrise for the process and the sun don't set here."

"Well, I don't see why we don't do it this way more often!" Michael laughed. "Seems like this is the best for everyone, right, Trip?"

Trip led him to the golf cart and shook her head. "The red stag's price isn't something to trifle with. We can't die in this area again, not until the sun is finally setting and rising again."

Michael turned to Trip, the smile falling off his face. "What did you trade? If it is too much—"

"Nothing is too much." She smiled slightly, squeezing his hand. "Nothing is too much if it keeps you here with me. Don't worry about it. We just have to be careful with our lives, and all I have to do is get to Horizon City and see the Sun King before two weeks are up."

Noel scrunched his nose, looking up at the sky, "In that case, we might need a bit of a short cut. We are awful close, but if we have a time limit, we need to hurry to be really safe."

Noel picked up his sister and helped her into the golf cart while she said, "Don't worry, Trip! The Sun King is super nice. I'm sure if you ask, you can see him right away."

Trip forced a smile on her face and nodded. "If you say so, Nevaeh."

Michael hunched over and started to cough, the sound rattling deep in his lungs. A minute later, two bullets popped out of his mouth. "Any chance we can take a slight detour? I'd really like to give this back to their proper owner."

Noel and Nevaeh let out a whoop and pumped their fists in the air. Noel said, "Let's make those assholes bleed."

As Nevaeh said, "That's what they get for hurting one of ours."

Trip's protest was drowned out by the blood lust of her fellow Trues. She understood it all too well. She wanted to slam her heel into Duvall's head over and over for putting her in this position. But did they really have time?

Noel shifted the golf cart in gear and they took off down the road, back towards the direction the Strikers left hours before. They drove for what felt like hours until they got to the outskirts of the Strikers' outpost. Trip twisted both of her hands off and grabbed two handguns. Noel and Nevaeh pulled out their handguns as Michael released a burst of energy, his blue fighting garments appearing as eyes released from the pattern on top. He held the bullet close to one of the eyes. In a moment, the eye split apart and ate it whole. The eye flashed and turned silver and grew a bit bigger, pointing in one direction no matter where Michael shifted. He smiled and signaled the Trues into camp.

They went in guns glazing, lasers were flashing with quick pulses from the eyes on Michael's shoulders, cutting into strikers before they had a chance to react. They destroyed the camp and those in it, until Michael found Duvall. The silver eyes focused right on him and

     DREAM OF THE SPIRIT MAN

shot a laser of shimmering silver, blasting right through his chest. As he toppled over, his face was frozen in an expression of shock and surprise, locked there in death.

Trip ran over to Duvall's body and kicked it, again and again before Michael pulled her off of him and said, "It's okay, Trip. He's gone. He won't hurt any of us again."

She kicked towards Duvall again and collapsed sobbing into Michael's chest. "If it wasn't for him…. I don't know if I can do it, Michael. I don't know if I can do it."

"If you can do what? Stop kicking a dead man?"

Trip looked up at Michael and said, "The red stag asked me to kill the Sun King. He gave me two weeks. But if I don't do it, you'll die and you won't come back. I can't lose you again."

He cupped her face and rested his forehead on hers. "Trip, no matter what you decide, I will back you up. I know why you didn't tell the twins. That's probably for the best. I don't want you to lose anything because of me. But if you decide to kill him, you can blame me. Or I can pull the final trigger."

She shook her head, tears flowing out of her eyes. "The stag said me. I don't want to accidentally have you end up dead. It's my burden. It was my deal."

She took a deep shaking breath and smiled. "Thank you. Thank you for being there for me and being so kind. I will do what I need to in order to keep you." Trip broke away, a bit red and blotchy and said, "Please don't tell the twins what I have to do. I want them to think well of me, and I know they care for the Sun King."

Michael nodded, and she left, walking back to the golf cart.

Guilt stabbed at Michael right between the ribs. Trip had said that she needed to leave as quickly as possible for Horizon City and instead he had them go backwards for revenge.

Michael found the twins in the middle of gathering some parts and putting it in the back seat of the golf cart. "We need to get going."

Noel waved his hand and kept working on tossing bits of metal in the compartment. "I'm making something for Nevaeh."

"Can you finish putting it together later? We need to get to Horizon

City as fast as we can."

Noel looked up, a bit shocked at the urgency in Michael's voice, and nodded. "Yeah, I can. Sorry, I forgot we were in a hurry. We can leave right away."

Michael smiled as everyone piled into the golf cart and they took off towards the horizon.

Chapter 21

When they stopped to rest three days later, Noel started pulling metal out of the back seat of the golf cart, fiddling with it a bit, and then put it back. He kept going over to his sister and measuring this and that. Nevaeh was telling a story of fighting a giant sea monster that Trip told her about when she was little, and Noel was bouncing on his toes, trying to wait for a good spot to cut in.

Nevaeh was clearly messing with her brother for a bit, adding extra words to the tale and spinning the story longer and longer until Noel couldn't stand it anymore and grabbed her hand. "Nevaeh. I made something for you."

She smiled, and he helped her to the cart. "I know you find it kind of frustrating you can't walk on your own due to lack of knees. So, I made you something. Two somethings actually."

He pulled out two metal contraptions and a wheelchair. "You can choose which one you like, or if the first one doesn't work, you can still get along by yourself if you need to!"

Nevaeh rolled her eyes. "Can you just tell me what it is that you made already?"

He gestured to the contraptions and back to her, stuttering a bit before clearing his throat. "You don't have knees, but you can still control the lower parts of your legs. Well, this combines the two. It can help so you don't focus as much and can still walk around."

"You made me artificial knees."

He looked at her and back at his contraption and then back at her. "They are a bit more complicated than that, but kind of. There is this whole latching mechanism that you have to do in order to kick some ass, but it should help. But—"

Nevaeh threw her arms around her brother and pulled him tight. "Thank you. It's wonderful, Noel."

He turned bright red and hugged her back tightly. "If they aren't comfortable or don't work as well as they should, I could make some adjustments but I—"

"They are perfect, Noel! Can you teach me how to put them on?"

Noel beamed and brought them over. It looked a bit like a metal brace, with small pieces of random cloth surrounding the parts where the metal would touch flesh.

But with a bit of practice, Nevaeh could walk again. She tried running but stumbled. Trip caught her before she hit the ground and said, "Just a bit more practice and you'll have that down."

Nevaeh ran as much as she could whenever they took a break, so happy to be able to move on her own again. It was like she'd gotten a second life, Michael reflected.

The next week, Michael and the Trues were in the middle of white sand dunes that stretched as far as the eye could see. Noel kept insisting he knew where he was going, and Michael could only trust him. What other choices did they have? All he could do was trust, right? Wasn't that what Trip had said?

They drove until they made it to a steel tower that stretched high into the sky. It had to be at least one hundred feet tall. It didn't have walls but was a frame of crossing metal bars. Several long metal chains hung down from the top of the tower.

The golf cart came to a rolling stop only feet from the base of the steel tower. In the distance, they heard a rumbling. General Bones was hunting them down. His army wouldn't stop until they killed the Spirit Man and the band of Trues once and for all. General Bones didn't want Michael to find the girl with three eyes. But more than anything, he hated that they spread hope and the will to fight. He didn't want Michael to save anyone, in this world or the next. And finally, he believed destruction was the truest form of salvation.

Michael could sense the evil intent in the air like a miasma across the desert, stretching back to Bones and his army. "They are coming for us," Michael whispered, trying not to give away their position to the warriors hunting them down. "We must be strong and brave. We can't let fear fester."

     DREAM OF THE SPIRIT MAN

A single bat demon flew fast toward them, holding a basket in his hands. As the demon flew towards them, great fear clung at Michael's heart. In this land, death stuck. Maybe there were answers in Horizon City, but it wouldn't help if they didn't get there. Michael didn't want Trip and the twins to feel his fear in case it might cause their own strength to falter.

The bat demon's wings caught the air and slowed down. He stopped yards away from Michael, landing solid on the ground with the basket held in front of him. He tossed the basket toward Michael and spread his wings wide, flying into the air. "Kill a demon and a hundred more take their place," the demon cried in a high-pitched, screeching voice. With two beats of his wings, he vanished into the horizon.

Michael and the trues all turned toward the basket, waiting for something. An explosion? Was this a threat? A peace offering? That wasn't likely.

"What was that about?" Noel said.

Nevaeh laughed and ran over, bending down to look at it.

"Be careful!" Trip yelled.

Nevaeh waved off her concerns and ran back to the golf cart, pulling out a long stick from the golf cart's back set compartment and then ran back, poking it with the stick. When it didn't do anything, she used the stick to flick the top open.

She shifted closer, peering inside and then laughed. "There is nothing inside!"

Trip ran over to the basket and grabbed it, looking inside. She flipped it around, pressing randomly into the weave. She growled and tossed it at Michael. "Did they just send this to mess with us? Why send a messenger with an empty basket?"

Michael shrugged and said, "Maybe it holds something humans can't see. Or it may come in useful later."

Noel crossed his arms and said, "I bet they are just trying to mess with us. Trying to throw us off our game before they try to finish us off."

Michael shook his head. "Whatever their reason, I say we don't let it get to us. We can just throw it in the golf cart and deal with it later."

Trip shrugged and said, "Might as well."

Michael glanced into the basket, but instead of nothingness, he saw a flash of colors. The worlds blended together, and the sun reversed in the sky, spinning and spinning until it froze like an unblinking yellow eye in the sky. Buildings reversed from dust to crumbling to full vibrant cities. There was a giant city, right here a long time ago. Ghosts of children ran past him, laughing and playing. People talked in a language he hadn't heard before, but he saw something that struck him. It was him, in dark blue shadow runner robes, laughing and talking with a bat demon. They were just sitting on a small wall, sharing a story. The moment froze and jumped forward, just enough that Michael caught snippets of what was happening before he was jolted back forward. A body, a young bat demon, crumpled on the ground. Outrage as both sides drew weapons on the other, the city split in two. A bat demon in a deep cave, chanting over a cauldron that flashed red. The city changing. The scenes flashed faster, so fast Michael couldn't really see more than an instant much less understand it. Battles. People crying, their hands over their eyes. Shadows. Blood. Death. So much death on both sides.

Then in an instant, he was back in the present, but Trip and the twins weren't moving. A girl with three eyes sat on nothing in the air and laughed. "You think you can fix things without realizing the cause? The answers you seek lie in the past."

Michael lunged forward, only for the girl to disappear and reappear in a different spot. "The universe must be balanced. Everyone must play their parts. The sun must set. The moon must rise. You must die. Again and again until you find what is needed. Until you heal the past."

Michael stopped lunging for her, just looking up at the girl with three eyes. "Please, I need your help."

"Of course you do. You can't do what you need to without me. But it will take more than this for me to help you. You have much more to do." She winked at him with her third eye, the amusement in her

     DREAM OF THE SPIRIT MAN

voice upsetting. Michael wanted to grab her and shake her for playing games with them like this, but even if he could, he knew it could
only go badly to lecture a god, no matter how little she was.

Michael spun, trying to catch the fleeting image of the girl before
she vanished and reappeared once more. "Please, what can I do?
Help me, please!"

She was moving faster now, her laughter echoing all around him.
"Find the center of three crossroads where the blood runs red. Grab
the petals long forgotten. Forget and remember."

She appeared right in front of him, glowing as the tips of her dress
drifted around her. "But for now, set the path right and fight." She
poked him in the center of his forehead and vanished.

Michael stumbled back, the force of one of her fingers stronger
than he had felt from a full arm. Time picked back up at a regular
speed, with Trip and the twins looking at him strangely.

Trip tilted her head and said, "What was that about? You just suddenly jumped like someone goosed you from beyond the grave."

Michael blinked, closing the basket's lid. "A lead for the future.
Hope? I don't know. I saw a lot and it was confusing. Sarah Eyestone
exists and told me a few more clues to finding her. We can do this.
But first, we have a battle to win."

Chapter 22

Michael looked off as a dust storm swelled in the distance, no doubt caused by General Bones and his army. Huge clouds rose above the western horizon that dripped in red. Thunder cracked and blue lightning streaked in the skies. Rain started to pour from the clouds, splashing bits of red and orange pigment on their faces.

"There has to be several thousand of them." Trip whispered hoarsely, looking out on the army with an expression of grim weariness.

"We can do it," Michael said, the eyes on his shoulders rising into the air and aiming all around him.

"We don't have anywhere to run, Michael," Trip said, a bit more urgently.

"We won't need to." Two of the eyes burned and when he touched them, one sword came out of each.

"Michael!" Trip yelled, yanking him towards her. "We can't do this."

Michael put one of the swords down and took her hand in his. "We have to. There is no other way through this crowd. Listen. You three mean more to me than this whole world does. What would you suggest, that we just lie down and die? We have to get up and fight, no matter the odds. We can't let them win. No matter what. I won't accept any other alternative."

Trip looked him in the eyes and smiled. She pulled him close and kissed him. "Let's give them a good fight then."

Michael grinned and picked up the sword he put down, watching as the twins armed up and Trip transformed. She took a deep breath and turned to the twins, putting her hands on the twins' shoulders. "I want you both to know I love you. That you make me so damn proud each and every day. Be careful. You got this."

She ruffled their hair and turned away as she unscrewed her

hands so they wouldn't see the emotions that threatened to escape. Noel tugged on her shirt and when she turned around, he said, "Trip, there is a reason I took us here. There should be a portal somewhere in the tower. A door that should lead us right to Horizon City." His eyes were bright. "If we can just survive one more battle, we'll be able to get into the city soon. Our journey is almost over."

"Really?" Trip said. She turned to Michael and saw him nod. She smiled and knelt down, looking right into Noel's eyes. "Then I want you to find it. Nevaeh, you should go too, Noel will need as much help as possible."

The twins nodded and took off, climbing a set of stairs that was on the outside of the tower looming over the field.

Michael glanced back at Trip. "Sent them away so they have a better chance?"

Trip looked up, wiping a tear from her eyes. "Might have diminished ours a bit, but I think it's worth it. Any chance we can keep the army off long enough for the twins to find the portal and get out of here?"

Michael nodded grimly. "We have to. To keep them safe, we'll have to buy them as much time as they need."

Trip nodded and cocked both of her guns, holding them up in front of her, aiming into the army. "Then bring it on."

The first part of the army that reached them were crazed bloodthirsty beasts that tried to rip out their throats, snarling as they lunged. Michael slid his swords into the belly of one creature after another, slicing right through them. Trip aimed, fired, and moved on, trusting her aim enough not to look at her enemy again once the bullet left her gun. The lasers on their shoulders came to life, blasting this way and that. The lasers defended them and each other. After the beasts fell, the animals dissolved and twisted into tiny bats. The bats took to the sky and beyond while Michael cursed. Why did they get another chance in this world when Michael and the Trues didn't without paying some awful price?

But he didn't have much time to think before the next wave descended, the army crashing into them. Gun fire erupted around them as Trip grabbed the small disk in her pocket and threw it into the air where it transformed into the Silver Disk, spinning and shooting into the bloodthirsty masses.

Trip jumped over bodies as they were falling to fire a volley into the next creature she could see.

General Bones shouted over his army, "Where are the rest of them? We must burn them all! Bring the device."

Something huge shifted out of the middle of the army. It looked like a semi-truck crushing anything and everyone in its way. But what was more shocking was what it was carrying. There was a gadget that was about ten feet long and six feet in width. Wires curled out of it, this way and that, but Michael knew what it was. It was a bomb, and a powerful one at that.

"Trip! Bones has a bomb on the semi," Michael yelled.

Trip turned and paled when she caught sight of the giant weapon. Michael had never seen a bomb so big, not even in the wildest movie. This one looked big enough to destroy everything in a single moment of fire and ash.

"That could blow up the entire desert! I'm on it. Keep them from the twins. Can you do that on your own?" Trip yelled, firing a non-stop barrage of bullets into the fray.

Michael nodded, sliding a blade into a Striker before spinning and slicing at another.

Trip ran over toward the semi and shot a path as she went. The demon driving the semi was cackling as he drove over hill and friend alike. Its grin dripped with black slime as it caught sight of Trip, shifting the semi into a higher gear and turning to ram her. She jumped out of the way, just in time, clinging to the back of the semi. She climbed up to the bomb. The demon noticed her climbing the bomb and took a sudden right, swinging her off of the side. Trip clung as tightly as she could. She pulled a knife out of her boot and started slicing at wires, pausing intermittently to hold on tight so she wouldn't be flung off.

Meanwhile, Michael was getting overwhelmed holding the line on his own. He was almost pushed all the way back to the tower. His

　　　　　DREAM OF THE SPIRIT MAN

swords spun and sliced, but there was only so much one person could do by themselves.

Trip finished tugging wires out as the light on the bomb flickered out and died. She grinned and started climbing for the driver. She climbed to the driver's side and punched through the glass, shot the demon and yanked the steering wheel so the semi careened toward a large portion of the army. As she was preparing to jump off, a bullet grazed past her arm and she fell onto the ground below.

Michael saw this and yelled, "Trip!" He started running toward her but stopped, spying the twins crawling higher in the tower. He had to stay and protect them. That was what he'd promised to do.

How dare this army try to take everything he cared about? If it wasn't for this senseless fighting, they wouldn't have to keep running. The twins could have had a normal childhood. Trip would be alive and well. Michael and she could even have a future together, if it wasn't for all this.

Eyes started vanishing from his outfit, and with each one that disappeared, the two eyes on his shoulders grew. Michael screamed in anguish and huge beams shot out from the eyes on his shoulders, leveling wave after wave of his enemies before he fell to his knees, exhausted.

"Trip." Her name left his lips in a whisper.

Michael had wiped out a good portion of Bones' soldiers, but there was still a huge army advancing toward him and the twins. He struggled to his feet and took a deep breath. He couldn't waste everything he had worked towards in his anger. He had to protect the twins. The two eyes shrank back down and the other eyes reappeared and opened together. He picked up his swords and started swinging, determined to keep the twins safe until they reached the portal. Then he might level the whole place himself.

The army halted in front of him and General Bones rode forward. "Give up, Spirit Man. Lay down your weapons."

"Why should I? I think I'd rather end you right here and now," Michael snarled.

General Bones laughed, "Bring the girl here."

A bat demon flew up toward the front of the army, a body in his arms. He landed right next to General Bones and said, "The Lady Dream Tripper."

Michael's shoulders burned, the laser focusing on Bones. Bones smiled and shook his head. "I didn't think you would want to be responsible for her death. She breathes still. Are you willing to stand by while I stop her? You still have a chance to save her. Put. Your. Weapons. Down."

Michael's swords dropped as he looked, but he still held onto the hilt. "Prove it. How could she have survived a fall like that? I saw…" He gulped, thinking of the way she'd fallen, how she looked like a doll from a distance. "…I saw what happened," he finished finally, his voice choked.

General Bones laughed. "Spending all your time chasing after a god and yet you know nothing of them. Dream Tripper isn't human. Lesser minds might even call her a god in her own right."

"Will you keep her alive? If I surrender?"

Bone's smile grew, and he shrugged. "It depends on how much longer you make me wait."

Michael's swords fell to the ground as Noel's head peaked out of the top of the tower. "Michael! It's up here."

Demons snatched Michael's swords as some held him down while General Bones laughed. "Bit too late, Spirit Man. Should I kill her first, or should I hunt down the twins and make sure you know their deaths are on your head as well?"

Michael lunged toward General Bones, even as the demons held him back. "You asshole! We made a deal. Let her go."

General Bones shrugged and said, "If only you hadn't made me wait. But to be honest, I was going to kill her no matter what you did. I've been waiting for this moment for far too long."

He pulled out a gun and aimed it at Trip. A shot went off, and Trip dropped. General Bones smirked and turned to Michael, but he could just watch in awe as Trip got up off the ground, her hands returning from behind the bat demon that held her. She shot him and he ended up taking both shots. Trip was fine.

Passion flamed inside Michael and he turned to his captors, the eyes flaring up again and blasting through his captors. General Bones spun around, unable to keep up as the two Trues kept demolishing his army until Trip found her way over to Michael. She smirked and said, "Knew you needed me. Can't fight by yourself for a few minutes while I'm away."

He reached out and touched her shoulder, for just an instant. Something to make sure what he saw was real. She smiled and turned back to the battle. Michael grinned, too. Seeing her alive and well put the wind back in his sails. He swung his swords as he said, "Noel found the gate. What's the plan now?"

Trip's eyes gleamed as she shot through enemy after enemy. "Try and follow. If not, blow the ever-living hell out of this place so these assholes can't follow them."

Michael smiled at her and let off another big blast from his shoulders. The moment the laser cut off, he ran toward the stairs with Trip. She faltered and checked the wound on her arm. It was still bleeding pretty badly, but she kept pushing on.

Michael kept shooting behind them when he noticed her stumble. "You're hurt?"

"No. I miraculously instantaneously heal when I get shot," Trip snapped impatiently.

"Why didn't you tell me?"

"Because like hell I'm going to slow you down."

Michael huffed. "Then you need to watch our backs," Michael said and swung her over his shoulder before taking the stairs as fast as he could. She shifted around a bit before turning around and firing down on the approaching army.

They could just hear as General Bones ordered his army to bring them back.

Michael climbed the stairs as fast as he could, finally spotting the twins. Noel and Nevaeh were aiming down the side of the tower, hitting as many demons as they could from their height. Michael waved them on. "Go through the portal! We'll be right behind you."

Noel looked like he was about to protest when Nevaeh grabbed him and pulled him along after her through the blue door.

"We need to find a way to keep the army from following us," Michael yelled. "Is there any way we can do that?"

Trip smiled and put her guns away, pulling a bomb out of thin air. "Kept enough supplies for this baby. Didn't know when we would need it most, but this feels right." She tossed it to the ground and Michael jumped through the blue door.

General Bones screamed as his army panicked, several getting trampled as others tried to escape. He lunged toward the door and flung it wide as the bomb hit the ground with a loud thud. The explosion took out the bottom of the tower and sent General Bones through the door, the door disintegrating as the explosion passed over it. A huge mushroom cloud erupted, vaporizing everything nearby.

Chapter 23

Waves of color soared past Michael and the trues as they were pulled through space. The inside of the door stretched for what looked like miles, swirling around them. Michael could see Noel and Nevaeh just a bit ahead, holding hands. There was a distortion that rippled through the portal and Michael turned. General Raven Bones was soaring towards them, getting closer and closer. Michael swung and punched him right out of the portal.

General Bones howled as he fell through the walls, sending him who knows where.

Michael and Trip caught up to Noel and Nevaeh and they clasped hands. They fell through clouds of dust and gas as they plunged downward. They spun out of control as they fell into a pit of darkness. While still holding hands, a miracle on its own, they hit something solid. A huge blinding flash of light exploded. There was another flash of blue light as they all jerked up from the ground, panting for air.

"What just happened?" Trip yelled. Her hands darted to her own face and then she jumped to her feet to check the twins over.

Michael shrugged and got to his feet. "Looks like we're somewhere else. Did everyone see that light or was it a dream?"

Nevaeh climbed to her feet and rolled her eyes. "It was both. And we told you where we were going."

Noel struggled to his feet and laughed as snowflakes started falling all around them. They were surrounded by blue doors of all shapes and sizes. They circled around them, more doors behind the ones that were closer in ever growing circles. The door right behind them was a normal size, but there were some that were only a foot or so tall and square, or eight feet tall but comprised of zigzags. But in the center, there were two doors. They were about five feet tall and faced each other. Both had two words etched in swirling cursive burned into the door. "Nevaeh's door" and "Noel's door," they read.

"Where are we?" Michael asked.

Noel shrugged and said, "This is home."

Nevaeh shook her head and said, "This is a middle ground. Most if not all blue doors lead here. The main question is figuring out where the others go. We try to label them, but they don't always lead to the exact same place."

"Which door leads to Horizon City?" Trip asked, her eyes wide as she tried to absorb all that she saw.

Michael took a step toward the doors in the middle when Noel jumped in front of him, arms out wide. "Don't!"

Michael put his hands up and stepped back. "I—"

Noel turned red and looked away. "That's ours. It's just for us. Please, don't ask."

Michael nodded, and Nevaeh cleared her throat and pointed at a door with a rounded top. "This door will take us to Horizon City. Not the one that leads to the Moon Queen's quarters, 'cause there might be a trap there. But this will get us close."

Nevaeh opened the door and took a step back. "You got to take a running step for this one, or you won't make it."

Nevaeh broke free from the others as she ran like a deer toward the magical door. She leapt through the air and vanished as she passed the threshold of the door. First Trip, then Noel, then Michael ran toward the door and leaped into the void.

The world shifted instantly, from the soft forest with a thousand doors to a bustling city. Michael blinked as he was thrown forward over a cliff surrounding the door they jumped through. He stumbled over the other side and crashed into a building on the other side. Noel and Nevaeh burst out laughing while Trip masked her snickering with her hand. Michael dusted himself off and smiled, taking in the sights of the city around them. Most of the buildings were made of adobe, one story with bright flags and ribbons connecting one house to the next. The city was alive with the sounds of joy and laughter and the occasional party. Animals and people walked around in colorful attire with smiles painted on their face. They pulled Michael and the Trues by their arms and began to dance. Music filled the air with beating drums and flutes.

Michael was spun out and spun closer again, only for the moose he was dancing with to whisper, "Help us."

For the first time, Michael caught sight of the citizens' eyes. They were empty and scared. The moose's mouth was still as he glanced behind them up to the blue castle behind them. The moose spun around so Michael could see. The palace was magnificent but a bit too perfect. There were two towers on opposite sides of the castle, one with a swirled sun painted on the side and the other with a moon. The towers stretched into the sky like menacing monsters. Shivers crawled up Michael's spine as he danced with the moose.

The sun tower's balcony caught Michael's eyes as a figure darted inside, causing the curtains to rustle.

Michael turned to the moose to ask a question, but he just smiled and started leading the dance somewhere else. Michael noticed that other animals were leading the others through dance to somewhere as well.

They danced into a house and danced into a room in the back that had no windows. When the door closed, the citizens stopped dancing and stopped pretending to smile.

Michael looked around and said, "What is happening here?"

The moose sat down on the ground, his head drooping. "Everyone under the sun must be happy. It is J.C. Blackstone's decree. The joy of the people is supposed to bring joy to the Sun King. But still, the sun has not set since the Moon Queen died. Some think that the king will not rest until the killer is found and caught. But most don't care. The heat burns us into dust as we do not rise with the rising of the sun. Death clings to our skin and yet we can only hope."

A small squirrel ran a paw over her whiskers and said, "The King is dying, but it may not be soon enough. The world is burning and there might be no one left to wake before the sun sets."

An ostrich flapped their wings and said, "But we have heard of you. The Spirit Man and his Trues. You can make things right again."

The squirrel nodded. "Convince the king to let the sun set. Stop Blackstone from whispering death into his ear."

"Help us," the moose said with sad eyes.

Michael stepped forward and said, "We are here to do just that. But we need a way into the castle. Do you know any way we can go in?"

The animals shook their head, eyes turned downcast. "We know none," the moose said. "The entrances were closed off. Blackstone is looking for the children who saw the queen last. Only their entrance is still open, and only because they hope to use it to catch them."

Nevaeh flinched and looked away. Trip looked around and said, "The kids know the entrance, but I'm not going to send them into danger."

The moose said, "The girl does not need to be the one to go through the door."

Nevaeh groaned and hid her face in her hands. "Who would be willing to do that for us?"

The squirrel stepped forward, her tail twitching. "I can go in first and draw them away. Then you can open the door."

Nevaeh looked around the room and turned a bit red. "That's good, but I don't want the others to know where the door is."

The squirrel glanced at her companions and smiled. "That's fine. Lead the way."

The ostrich shifted their feathers and said, "We will lead you to the servant's entrance. Follow me." The ostrich reached for the door handle but paused. "You must not let out any unhappy emotion in the sunlight. Smile and dance."

Michael nodded, and they took off, following the animal they chose, dancing and swinging and laughing in different directions.

Hours passed as Michael and the moose danced by the servants' entrance only to leave again when a guard came walking by.

He traded a worried glance with Trip who was a bit too far away to talk to.

The moose smiled and said, "It is almost the mandatory sleeping hours. We can only dance for so long before happy dreams."

Michael glanced at the door and shook his head, forcing a smile on his face. "We should do one more dance before."

"I don't know if that is a good idea," the moose said, tilting his head to a nearing guard.

Just then there was a slight shift in the door knob. Michael and the moose started dancing toward the door when the guard stopped in front of them. "Just what are you doing out when it is time to sleep?"

Michael's head spun as he tried to think of a good reason, a happy thought when Noel jumped forward with a big smile on his face. "We were just so happy to be in this town. We traveled a long way and wanted to enjoy as much of it as possible! We couldn't possibly sleep when we are this close to a god!"

The guard grinned and said, "Oh, you're tourists! That's great! Feel free to stay out a bit longer and enjoy the sights. But do go to bed soon, the city is gorgeous at daybreak."

The guard continued walking on, but the moment he was out of sight, Michael, Trip, and Noel darted toward the door. Michael smiled and ruffled Noel's hair. "Good thinking! I was sure we wouldn't get another chance until tomorrow and that would be a bit too late."

The animals waved as Michael and the Trues darted inside to a dark kitchen. The squirrel darted outside and Nevaeh crashed into Trip's arms. "I wasn't sure you guys would be able to come through in time! I'm sorry it took some time; the guards just wouldn't leave and I—"

Trip kissed the top of her head and said, "It's okay, Nevaeh. You did good! We're in now and that's what matters. It should be smooth sailing until we find the Sun King."

The lights flickered on and revealed a man sitting in the corner. His hair was black and slicked back, his eyes like coals and his goatee pointed at the ends. He got to his feet and smiled while walking towards them, a knife gleaming in his hands. "Welcome, Trues. I'm J.C. Blackstone. Might I ask how you got into the castle?"

<h1 style="text-align:center">Chapter 24</h1>

Blackstone looked over the group and his eyes landed on the twins. He jumped to his feet and ran over, freezing when the twins recoiled back from him. He knelt down and said, "You're okay? I was so worried. You disappeared, and everyone said you killed the queen, but I knew that couldn't be true."

Nevaeh stepped in front of her brother, pulling out a gun and aiming at the magician. "Of course that isn't true. You killed the Moon Queen."

Blackstone put a hand to his chest and looked up at Michael and Trip before turning back to the twins. "What are you talking about? I loved the queen, why in the world would I kill her?"

Noel crossed his arms and glared at him. "Don't lie. Nevaeh saw you."

Blackstone's hands fell to the ground as he thought for a minute. "Something doesn't make sense. I heard you did it. But you say you saw me do it? I don't know what's going on," he said, looking up with a sudden determination in his eyes, "but I will find out. If there is anything I can do to prove my innocence to you, I will do it."

Noel rolled his eyes. "If you really want to prove your innocence, you can give Nevaeh her knees back."

Blackstone paused and turned to examine Nevaeh's knees. "They are gone. What happened?"

Nevaeh glared at him and said, "What do you mean, what happened? You were there. I kicked you in the gut and you ripped my knees off."

Blackstone put his hands up and said, "From what I know of the Trues' magic, it leaves a residue. Do I have the residue on me? Can you tell?"

Trip squinted and shook her head. "He doesn't. And that isn't something you can just get rid of. Seems like he is telling the truth."

Michael put his gun down and said, "Then tell us what you know about the Sun King. We need to get to him." This was all confusing, but they needed to get to the bottom of things in order to let Trip keep her promise and get Nevaeh's knees back from…well, from whoever it turned out had stolen them.

Blackstone stood up and dusted himself off. "He is in his tower. He has not left it since the queen died. I will lead you to the tower and past the guards, but I do not know what his reaction to seeing the twins will be."

Nevaeh crossed her arms and huffed. "He'd be happy to see us. He knew we wouldn't do something like that."

Blackstone shook his head but started walking, leading the way. "The Sun King hasn't been in the right mindset for a while. There is no telling anymore what he would do. Please, follow me."

Trip pulled out one of her handguns and said, "If you try to lead us into a trap, we will kill you. And even you should know what will happen then."

Blackstone nodded and started walking. "As I said, I am willing to do anything for the twins to trust me again. And I do know of the problems." Blackstone rubbed the bridge of his nose and sighed. "The king has been neglecting his duty for a while. The queen did what she could, but the sun must set. The land needs rest. Sleep helps the mind restore, and this land hasn't been able to truly rest for a while."

Blackstone led them out of the kitchen down a long hallway, pausing periodically to avoid the guards. He continued, "The people are dying and there is nothing I can do to stop it. Only a god can stop a god, but the world needs sunlight as well as moonlight. The way things are going, there soon won't be either."

Noel said, "We are going to convince him to let the sun set again."

Blackstone chuckled, but no mirth was in the sound. "The Sun King wouldn't listen to me and his queen, much less to two twins who hid in his castle like rats to sneak in and find him in his privacy. Why would he listen to you?"

Noel stuck his chest out and said, "We have the Spirit Man and Dream Tripper with us. He'd listen to them if he won't listen to us."

Blackstone turned to Michael and Trip and hummed. "Well, perhaps the two heroes will change his mind. I must warn you, he may see them as a threat. Only one with such power can replace a god. Are you willing to take his place, Spirit Man and Dream Tripper?"

Michael looked over at the twins and Trip and shook his head. "I don't think I could. I need to continue my journey to find the girl with three eyes."

Blackstone nodded and said, "But surely it would be fine to rest for a while. Until a new god could be made or found. Think of it, a soft bed, good food, and not having to run or fight. You could rest."

Michael chuckled and said, "Sleep would be nice, but nothing would beat my own bed back in my own world. But I can't stop now. I have to continue, or what else will make me start again? Comfort leads to ignoring the plight of others. I need to help all I can so I can sleep comfortably at night in my own bed when this is done."

Nevaeh glared at her feet and snorted. "Well maybe you can find a way home after this adventure. If a chance opened now, would you leave us?"

Michael glanced at the ceilings, the ornate detailing carved into the wall, and then back at Trip and the twins. "I can't leave now. I need to help with the Sun King."

Nevaeh muttered something under her breath and Noel snorted. He whispered back to his sister, "Trust him."

Nevaeh rolled her eyes and said, "So what is the great plan to get the Sun King to change his mind? Blackstone makes it seem like we can't just walk in and talk to him. So, what do we do?"

Blackstone ran a finger over the edges of his goatee thoughtfully. "We could force the Sun King to do the ritual and have the sun set. But I do not know if it would be enough without the moon as well. Maybe for one day, but longer would be damaging in its own way. Besides, it would be hard to force him into the position day after day."

"Why doesn't he retire?" Michael asked. "It seems he really doesn't like his job. No wonder the other spirits are ticked off at him."

Blackstone hummed as he led them up the stairs and said, "Are they? Then we must hurry before they send someone to kill him. Regicide is not looked fondly on, even if it is done by a hero."

Michael and Trip exchanged a glance and Blackstone clapped. "We're here. We really should have a plan in advance though."

Trip squared her shoulders and said, "We have a plan. We're going to kill him."

Nevaeh gasped as Blackstone nodded and said, "I figured the gods would send someone."

Noel yanked on Michael's arm and growled, "I thought we were just going to talk to him! Why would we kill him? He hasn't done any-thing to us." Anger filled his words. "The Sun King was good to us! Why hurt him when he might just be a man in pain and grief?"

"That was the deal with the red stag," Michael said while Trip looked at her feet. "We have to kill him."

"We don't kill humans," Noel said, stomping his foot. "We kill bad guys like the demons and strikers. Bad guys."

Michael shrugged and said, "That's what the red stag asked for. If we don't, I'm gonna die again and nothing can bring me back."

Nevaeh looked through him as she said, "Why didn't you just tell us that? You lied to us. You said you just had to talk."

"We didn't know how you would react. Sometimes we have to do the hard thing," Trip said, trying to make her voice gentle.

Noel glared at Michael and Trip and said, "We do the right thing. We help people. We don't hurt those like us."

"What do you think the Strikers are?" Trip whispered, not look-ing the twins in the eye. "General Bones. The foot soldiers. I thought you knew."

"They are bad guys," Noel said slowly. "What do you mean?"

Trip shook her head and said, "They were just like us at one point. Hopelessness changes people and the gods tried to warn us before. But we didn't listen, so it spread. I can't let that happen again. I have to kill the Sun King."

Michael sighed and said, "You don't have to come in and see this.

But we have to do this. I'm sorry."

Michael opened the door and was blown back into the wall by a blast of heat. Through the doorway, an old man with gray hair stood, his finger steaming as it pointed at Michael, a gold crown on his head. "Look who you follow, children. Look how they lie and try to turn you against me. Join me as they burn for their transgressions."

<h1 style="text-align:center">Chapter 25</h1>

Nevaeh looked between the Sun King and Michael and stepped inside the door, standing beside the Sun King. He patted her face and said, "I knew you would make the right decision. Why would you stick with those who lied to you? Who tried to use you?"

Nevaeh pulled out her gun and aimed it at Trip and Michael, glancing at her brother with pleading in her gaze. "We can't trust them, Noel. Please."

Noel sighed and followed his sister. "I'm sorry, but I need to stay with her. But do you have to hurt them, Sun King? Can't you just do your job as the sun god?" He looked back at Michael and Trip, pain clear in his eyes. "I don't want them to get hurt any more than I want them to hurt you," he said softly.

The Sun King's laugh shook the room and he ruffled the kids' hair. "I don't control the sun. A bit of fire from my fingers and suddenly I'm responsible for the sun rising and setting. Pushed into a ridiculous repetitious monotony that stretched toward eternity. No more. I refuse."

Blackstone yelled through the door, "And the sun stopped! Are you really so cold that you ignore your people's suffering? That you don't let those they love come back to them?"

Fire blasted out of the Sun King's hand in a sudden burst, but Blackstone dodged behind the door. Fire erupted around the metal where the Sun King struck. "Why should they get their loves back when I can't get mine? Where was my queen when the sun rose again, only for her blood to be on your hands?"

Trip was focused on the Sun King and slowly unscrewed her left hand as Michael debated whether he should transform or not. The Sun King had the twins on his side. He didn't want to harm them if it was at all possible. But was it possible to leave this situation and hurt only the Sun King? Michael sighed, put his hand on Trip's shoulder, and shook his head. "It's not worth the chance of harming them."

Trip nodded and Blackstone blinked, shaking his head. "I thought you said the twins killed her. That's what you told the guards," he called into the Sun King's chamber.

The Sun King laughed and laughed, the sound echoing off the walls around them. "You always were smarter than you should have been." He adjusted his coat and changed shape, shifting into an exact replica of Blackstone. "She always did like spending time with you more. I thought she was just cheating on me, but it was much worse than I could have thought."

He shifted back to his normal form and blasted another fire ball toward Blackstone, who dodged behind a pillar. "You weren't doing your job! The people were suffering, and you didn't even try to help them," Blackstone cried.

The Sun King stalked closer and a fireball grew in his hand. "So, you decided to turn my wife against me? To try and poison me? She died because of your actions, even if not directly by your hand."

Nevaeh's eyes shot to the Sun King and she drew her gun and aimed it at him, her hand shaking. "So you killed her?" Her voice was high with betrayal. "You killed your own wife, the Moon Queen?"

The Sun King turned toward the kids and the fire in his hands flickered and faded. "What would you do if the ones you trusted lied to you? If they tried to kill you? Who knows where lies may lead?"

Nevaeh turned the gun back on Michael and Trip, who put their hands up again in surrender. They would not take up arms against her.

The Sun King threw a blast behind one of the pillars, but Blackstone had moved while he was distracted with the twins. Fire flared back in the palm of the Sun King's hand. "How much sweeter was it to use the very poison you were going to use on me? To see her lover's face as she died in his arms?"

The Sun King continued to taunt Blackstone while Michael tried to figure out how to get out of this situation. He had to keep the twins safe. But why had they switched sides? Maybe they should have told the twins the truth from the beginning. "Noel, Nevaeh," he cried to them across the room, "I'm sorry. We should have told you. We just wanted to protect you from the harshness this world brings. I would give anything for you to have a normal childhood, one where you didn't have to watch over your backs or learn the sounds of death. I didn't mean to hurt you. I'm sorry."

Nevaeh growled, "You didn't mean to hurt us? Well, tough luck, because lying fucking hurts. Why didn't you just trust us to do the right thing?"

Trip shook her head. "Sometimes the right thing isn't easy to see, much less to do. I didn't want the guilt on your heads. It was my decision to do this, to take the red stag's bargain. Please, don't blame Michael."

"He lied to us too. Do you really think you can pull off sweet thoughts like, 'I wish they had a normal childhood,' when it comes to a choice like this? As if any child in the DW gets a normal life. The world has been drenched in blood since before our birth because of chance. I learned to shoot a gun before I learned to write and read. Don't be a coward and simply wish for a better life for us. You have to work for it and help."

Michael sighed and said, "I... You're right. We should have asked you and seen your side."

Nevaeh snarled and said, "Too late for apologies."

The Sun King laughed loud and caught their attention. "And do you really think my death would set the sun spinning again? It stopped because it was tired of the heinous things we do to each other, and not because of anything I did. The other so-called gods can shove it if they think killing me will make a difference. It just tells me what weak minds I need to destroy next."

Michael rolled his eyes and shouted, "Gods exist, stupid. We've met them before."

The Sun King spun around to Michael at the same time Michael spotted Blackstone crawling over the ledge of the balcony, trying to scoot to another pillar. Michael needed to distract the Sun King for a bit longer. "I've met Lord Striker myself. And the lonely rider

Ace. The girl with three eyes came to me and told me what I needed to do for my quest. To say that gods don't exist doesn't make sense in a world where you can touch them."

The Sun King stalked toward Michael. "False gods can do many things. Who's to say that these weren't just powerful people with their own agendas? Power belongs on top, but to claim godhood is sin. Who is to say that the girl with three eyes did not simply try to distract you with a fruitless quest to keep anything from challenging her power?"

"Sarah wouldn't do that. We can help the world."

The Sun King laughed and said, "Oh really? What lies did she spin for you? That you were important? That you could succeed in your quest? All of these are lies she tells to anyone she can trap."

"How can you think that?" Michael asked.

His fist created a crater in the wall. "Because she told that to me. Happy marriage, happy life, if only I do the job she asked. If only I followed her without doubting the reasoning behind it. But all her promises are just lies."

Michael shook his head. "You didn't try. You stopped doing what she asked."

"Because the sun moved on! After being told you can move the sun, can you imagine the crushing disappointment when you forget one day and the sun keeps moving? It took one year for the sun to stop, to finally realize that I wasn't keeping it going anymore. Because it didn't need me, not really. It was all a fun trick for the little three-eyed god to play."

"You can't know! Maybe she gave you spare time. Maybe it's like winding a clock and things slowly stop. Maybe—"

"Maybe you are trying to explain a god who doesn't need you and just needs to keep you distracted from looking too deeply at the world around you."

Blackstone was almost on the other side. Michael shook his head and said, "Sometimes you need to have faith. Sometimes you need to try and try and try and it might feel like it's going nowhere. But other times, you see the good you did. A person coming back to life.

A friend saved because you happened to be in the right place at the right time. The gods chose me to help, and I have to do that. I have to help where I can."

For a split second, Michael thought that his distraction of the Sun King was working. One more move, and Blackstone would make it out just fine. Michael let out a small sigh of relief, but it was too soon to feel relief. The sun king laughed and turned, fire flaring up past his elbow as he slammed the fire through the pillar Blackstone was hiding behind. The room was filled with the roar of the fire, yet Blackstone's screams seemed to be the loudest thing Michael had ever heard. Then the screaming stopped just as quickly as it started. The sun king looked at his hand as Blackstone's charred body tumbled to the ground far below the window of the tower, a grin spreading across his face. "And sometimes, nothing you do can stop the inevitable."

Chapter 26

"Traitors always get what comes for them," the Sun King said, turning to Trip and Michael. "So, what other fate would await those who would attempt to commit such a sin?"

Noel stepped in front of Michael and Trip and said, "They were just doing as they were told, too. If you don't want to do your job as Sun King, we can find someone else. No one else has to die." His eyes lingered on Blackstone's body with a troubled look.

Trip paled and said, "The red stag specifically stated that the Sun King had to die. That I needed to kill him."

Noel rolled his eyes. "There is always a way around that. Crown a random bat demon king for the day and kill him. No one else here has to die."

Michael sighed and said, "Noel, he is hurting his citizens. He killed the Moon Queen and the magician. He is burning the world and he just threw his advisor over the side of the building."

Noel looked between Michael and the Sun King, something desperate growing in his eyes. "Please. There has been too many here who have died."

"Fine," Trip said, unscrewing one of her hands behind her back. "Do you agree to step down for the good of your people, Sun King?"

The Sun King laughed and laughed, the very air around him heating up and rippling. "You think I will step down? Those idiots think I'm a god, why would I let that go? They are willing to do whatever I ask. The city was so dull before but now they are singing and dancing every day! Don't tell me that's bad."

"They aren't dancing because they want to," Michael said. "They are dancing because you will kill them if they don't. That's not real happiness. Forced happiness isn't happiness at all."

The Sun King turned down the heat and held his hands out toward

Noel. "You have to choose your side. They aren't gods, they burn just like anyone else. Who took care of you while they disappeared? Who let you die and forgot you ever existed?"

Noel was shaking as Michael said, "He tried to put the blame of the queen's death on you and your sister. He took her knees."

Nevaeh's eyes narrowed as she turned to the Sun King, looking him over. "Trip, you said he would have a residue?"

Trip nodded. "It should glow if you get closer."

Nevaeh took a step closer to the Sun King and he shook his head, stepping back from her approach. "I should have known these false prophets would turn you against me. Worry not children, I will not hold it against you." He reached into his robes and flung two rings at each of the twins. The metal wrapped around their legs and arms before growing, dragging them to the ground. "That does not mean I will let you fight against me."

Trip drew her knife and lunged at the sun king. "What did you do to them?" she shouted. She swung her knife at him again and again but he dodged out of the way like it was nothing, laughing all the while. He spun, flipping her over and blasting her into the wall. Michael could hear the sound of something cracking, whether it was Tripp's bones or the wall, he couldn't be certain.

Michael ran over to check on her as the Sun King taunted them. "What did I do? I had to keep my scapegoats from fighting me before their trial. Killing the queen and then fleeing, trying to blame the mighty magician. When he caught them trying to go after me, he met his untimely demise. Fortunately, I was able to catch them and the false gods, the Spirit Man and Dream Tripper."

Nevaeh thrashed around in her restraints and screamed, "You asshole! You tricked us."

The sun king laughed and said, "Of course I did. Children are so easy to deceive. I don't blame your companions for attempting it." He swept toward the twins, pulling out a box from a desk nearby. When he opened the box, he started glowing softly.

Michael had scooped up Trip and held her close. He could see her chest heaving. A large sigh escaped him. She was disoriented, her eyes darting around the room, not focusing on anything. He hugged her close for a second before he set her down to join the fight. Michael charged the Sun King, summoning both of his swords as the Sun King barely dodged out of the way, tossing the box back into a corner. The mad king clapped his hands together and when he pulled them apart, a sword of flame appeared between his hands. Soon he was matching every blow Michael swung.

"I wonder," the Sun King began, "how happy the people will be when they find out their useless Spirit Man is dead."

Trip shifted and struggled to her feet, stumbling as she tried to fight the wave of vertigo. Michael transformed from one instance to the other, his blows coming faster. But the sun king was able to still block as he danced around the room. No matter what Michael tried to do, the Sun King seemed to know every move, and no different strategy or try at underhanded tactics was working. The Sun King swung and one of Michael's swords flung out of his hand. He could feel the rush of heat past his skin with every stroke, like small sunburns streaking across his body in random slashes. He was down to one sword and he wasn't making any progress with it. What could he do with only blade?

It seemed like the Sun King noticed the same thing. He laughed and said, "Do you really think you are powerful? That you can make a difference? Then why didn't your god with the three eyes save you when you died? Why did you need to trade with the red stag at all? You're replaceable. Admit it."

The Sun King gasped as a knife shoved through his shoulder, attached to one of Trip's disembodied hands. Trip swayed on her feet, stepping closer to the Sun King and Michael. "We can't know the will of the gods. But Michael and the twins aren't replaceable. They matter to me. Who cares whether our mission is blessed by the gods or cursed? It matters to us and that alone makes it important. We have to try to make the world better. And right now, that means a world without you."

Trip pulled the knife out and the Sun King collapsed on the ground. Trip's hand slowly screwed back into place, even as she crumpled

     DREAM OF THE SPIRIT MAN

into Michael's side. It seemed like every little movement was causing her pain, her breathing labored. He was barely able to hold her
up. Slowly, he lowered her to the ground before he ran to the box,
tossing Nevaeh her knees before struggling with the metal that
kept them locked up.

Nevaeh snarled, "Don't pretend to care now, liar."

Noel shifted, obviously uncomfortable, and said, "Nevaeh, he just
wants to help."

Michael glanced over at Trip and the Sun King and said, "If there
was anything I can do to make it up to you, I would. Please, we need
to get out of here and get a new Sun King as soon as we can. Trip
isn't doing good."

Nevaeh scoffed and said, "Really? You would abandon us in an
instant if you had the chance. You just said so to Blackstone. You just
want to go home to your soft bed and easy life where you don't have
to think about us."

Michael tugged at the metal, but it kept still, not moving. "I—"

The words froze in his throat as he caught Nevaeh's expression
of horror. Michael turned around and saw the Sun King get back up,
his bones jerking around under his skin, growing and shifting. His
arm swiveled around, bending in four places before popping into a
different place. A pained groan erupted from the Sun King's lips as
his face changed, accompanied by loud cracking sounds. His form
was getting bigger, but long black spikes shot out of his spine and
he was shoved to all fours. The sun king was turning into a monster
right in front of them. A giant tail swept from his spine, with spikes
pointing every direction.

"Did you really think that something so simple could kill a god?"
he said with a booming laugh as his body grew, his spikes breaking
through the roof above them.

Michael called up his lasers just in time, blasting through the roof
as pieces started to fall all around them.

"Perhaps my citizens would like a reminder of who they wor-
ship. But first," he said, smashing his tail through the roof before
crawling down the building to the sleeping city below, cackling all

the way. One giant piece of the roof started falling right toward the twins and Michael lunged as the twins screamed. The lasers turned the piece of the rubble into dust. The twins were still trembling as Michael said, "I'm sorry. I'll be right back. I need to take him out before he destroys the whole city."

Nevaeh looked away and said, "Go. We are good at taking care of ourselves."

"I know you can. But that doesn't mean you should have to. I'm sorry we hurt you. I'll be back as soon as I can. I promise." Michael glanced at the twins and the unconscious Trip once more before he took off to find the beast of a king.

Chapter 27

Nevaeh watched as Michael jumped over the edge of the tower's crumbling walls. She growled and thrashed, trying to figure out how to get out of her bonds. Noel was sitting down, head drooping, and Trip was slumped on the ground. Trip started moving a bit, her fingers twitching. "Noel, we need to get out of this mess."

"We can't get out on our own," Noel said. "Why would you send Michael away? He is the only one who can help us right now."

"We can help ourselves. We don't need him. Come on, you can think of something! You always figure something out," Nevaeh said.

Noel sighed and said, "It's okay to ask for help. It's okay to trust other people besides me. Michael and Trip didn't mean anything bad. They just wanted to protect us."

"I'm fine at asking for help. I just asked you, didn't I? And don't tell me you bought that stupid apology. If they really cared, they would have told us. We could have handled it."

"Really?" Noel asked, scooting closer to his sister. "What did you do the moment you found out? You turned against them."

Nevaeh ground her teeth together, scooting closer to Noel as well until she fell over. "They lied to us. Who knows what else they are hiding? We can't trust them again."

Noel finally made it over to Nevaeh and started messing with the brace on her left leg. "I'm not saying you have to forgive them. It's just, we won't get anywhere if we don't get help where we need it. And Michael and Trip are willing to help. We can leave as soon as we are safe if that would help you feel better. But right now, we need them. And they need us."

Noel pressed down on a button that would belong under her knee and the bottom of her leg separated. She slipped her left leg out of the restraints and then used her leg to push off the restraint on her right leg.

She crawled toward the area where Michael tossed her knees and closed her eyes before pounding the ground with her fists in frustration.

Noel twisted around and said, "What's going on? Why aren't you reattaching your knees?"

Nevaeh's head dropped and she sighed, "I can't move them. My knees might have been away from my area of influence for too long or something. I don't know."

"So what?" Noel said. "You are my sister. You can do amazing things whether your legs are attached with skin or metal. I believe in you."

Nevaeh picked up her knees before crawling back to the metal brace she left near Noel. She slipped it back on and gently tapped Noel's head with her own. "Thank you."

He smiled and said, "Please save our butts now, if you can."

Nevaeh struggled to her feet and said, "Of course."

She knelt down next to Trip, shaking her awake. Trip's eyes fluttered open and she smiled when she saw Nevaeh. "You're okay? That's a relief."

Trip's eyes closed again and Nevaeh shook her again. "Not quite safe yet. Any chance you can shift into that outfit with the lasers? I think that might be the only thing that can get this annoying contraption off."

Trip struggled to sit up and nodded. A burst of blue energy flowed around her, pulsing and settling into her skin, flickering. Trip shook her head and said, "I don't think I can hold it. Where is Michael?"

"He left."

Noel chimed in, "He went to go fight the monster the Sun King transformed into. Don't go making him sound like an asshole, Nevaeh."

Nevaeh rolled her eyes and said, "Same difference. He left and is gonna die and the Sun King will come back and finish us off."

Trip was pale but closed her eyes for a bit, focusing as much as she could. "I can only hold it enough for one good blast. I can't free you both right now."

"Free Nevaeh," Noel shouted. "I'll be fine."

Trip's head bobbed, and the eyes flickered into existence for a split second, sending out a controlled blast before disappearing again. Nevaeh pulled her wrists apart and went over to where her handgun had fallen. "Guess I can try to shoot you out of your restraints."

Trip shook her head weakly and whispered, "Please. Help Michael."

Nevaeh stomped her foot and said, "Why in the world would I want to help him? Maybe if we are lucky, the Sun King and Michael will just wear each other out and we won't have to mess with anything."

"You have to help him," Noel pleaded. "Michael is trying to save the world. But even if he doesn't get that far, he is trying to save the people of Horizon City. He is helping those who helped us, the same ones who are in danger because we failed to kill the Sun King before he rampaged. Please, Nevaeh."

Nevaeh groaned but cocked the gun. "Fine."

She started to walk toward the edge of the tower when she halted, her pants caught on something. Trip held onto her jeans, unscrewing one hand that she used to pick up a gun. Trip looked up at Nevaeh and said, "I need to be the one who kills him. Please, take my hand with you and use it to deliver the final blow."

Nevaeh growled and snatched the hand up. "Can you even control it from that far? You don't have anyone to boost your range and even if you did, it would still be a bit much."

Noel started scooting over to Trip and said, "I can be her boost. Just yell when you need to fire."

"Noel—"

He smiled up at her, leaning against Trip. "Please trust me. You got this. I believe in you."

Nevaeh tried to hide a smile but slipped. She nodded and took off down the tower.

The Sun King's new tail slammed into Michael's side, sending him into a nearby wall. He felt all the air leave his body and he saw stars. The only thing he could do was shake it off and focus on getting back up.

The Sun King laughed. "You can hold up better than the Dream Tripper did. Is that why you are trying so desperately to stop me now? Did she pass on?"

Michael pulled himself up again, holding tight to his sword before charging at the monster again. The monster smashed through a building and raked his claws against Michael's chest. Michael shouted, his chest burning from the claw marks, but it didn't stop him from going after the monster again. He needed to keep fighting.

"You are getting desperate," the monster taunted. "Maybe I can make you even more. It doesn't matter if you kill me now, the sun needs to set and rise again to bring people back to life. But the bodies need moonlight to rise, and you won't get that ever again. I hid that traitor's crown, so no one could find it again. Your precious people aren't coming back. No one is, ever again."

"I wouldn't underestimate my family," Michael said. "Trip and the twins are stronger than anyone gives them credit for."

The monster laughed and stomped on a building, crushing it under his weight, swinging his tail around to create more destruction. Citizens rushed out of their homes, distress obvious on their faces. "Look what you caused, Spirit Man. They were happy, and you brought their end. What will you do when you see those you wanted to save die in front of you and know that it was your fault?"

The monster charged forward, and Michael called upon all of his remaining strength and dove into the monster's side, tossing him off track. The monster laughed, picking Michael off his side with his tail and slamming him into the ground. "You can't even truly fight me because you are not the one who is supposed to kill me. Roll over and die, Spirit Man, and know you won't wake up again."

The monster lifted up his foot and was prepared to crush Michael when Nevaeh appeared, kicking the monster away from where Michael was. She jumped in front of Michael and stared the monster right in his eyes. "Don't touch my family." She pointed Trip's hand toward the monster and shouted, "Trip, now!"

The bullet shot through the monster's skull and his forward momentum sent him crashing down right at her feet. The monster shriveled and twitched, shrinking back down first in the shape of the Sun King, and then an older man. His crown fell off his head as he reduced to bones, a slim silver crown peeking out from between his ribs.

The people began to mutter as Nevaeh helped Michael to his feet. "Who is going to be the Sun King now? The sun must rise and set again. But who could hold such a power?"

She propped Michael up against a nearby wall and knelt down, picking up the golden crown in her hands before placing it on her own head.

Chapter 28

The crown rippled and shrank, fitting her head perfectly. The citizens watched in silence for a beat before bursting into cheers. Nevaeh ignored the sound and picked the smaller silver crown out of the Sun King's ribs. Michael turned back to the crumbling sun tower and said, "Trip and Noel?"

Nevaeh rolled her eyes and said, "They should be fine now. Got the crown, right?"

"The Sun King said the moon needs to rise as well." Michael said, struggling to stand on his own feet. "Besides, it would be best if they didn't die."

He turned to the crowd and said, "Is anyone here a doctor? We need help."

The citizens muttered to each other and a small duck stepped forward and nodded. "I can help. You saved us from the mad king, we will do whatever you need."

Nevaeh waved at the sun tower and said, "We have several people who are severely injured."

The duck waddled forward and said, "I will do what I can."

They made their way to the castle tower and Michael used the last of his strength to blast off Noel's restraints. The duck clucked as she worked over Trip and shook her head, turning to Nevaeh. "My liege, I am sorry, but your friend needs help I cannot give. Only the healing rays of the moon can help her, but with the Moon Queen dead, I'm not sure how to accomplish that."

Nevaeh pulled out the small silver crown and the duck covered her mouth. "The moon crown...you found it! But who will wear it? The person will be bound to the rituals and the land."

Michael turned to Trip with a sad smile. "If that's what is needed, that's what I'll do. I can't do this without Trip."

Nevaeh's eyes widened and she said, "But if you take the crown, you know you won't be able to go home again, right? You might not even be able to finish your quest for the girl with three eyes. You'd be stuck."

Michael nodded and stared at the sky. "I know. But I can't lose any of my family. She would do it for any of us in a heartbeat."

He stepped forward, reaching for the silver crown, when Noel snatched it out of Nevaeh's hands. The boy grinned and said, "Can't go stopping now. You need to continue on your quest. You need to be able to go home."

"Are you sure?" Michael asked. "We don't know what this means. What it will take to make the sun and moon rise."

Noel smiled and said, "I'm not leaving my sister. Besides, this might lead to that slightly more normal childhood that you wanted for us. We can do this."

Michael shook his head. "You don't have to stick to this. Maybe you can pass on the power to someone else. We don't even know if transferring the crowns would transfer the powers and responsibilities."

Nevaeh laughed and snapped, a small flame appearing over her hands. "I think it does."

Noel smiled and put the crown on his head. The crown glowed ever so slightly, shrinking down to fit Noel's head perfectly. He closed his eyes and a beam of light shot into the sky. The power faded and he dropped to his knees, a soft smile on his face as he looked up at the sky. Where the beam landed, there was now a full moon rising over the clouds.

Nevaeh frowned and said, "Well, that's good, but I have to admit I have no idea how to make the sun go down."

The duck stepped forward, wings pulled in front of her. "The Sun King used to do the rituals in public every morning and night. I can tell you what he did, if you think that would help?"

Nevaeh nodded and the duck said, "Well, for the sun to set, I think you have to be focused or centered or something. The Sun King always sat facing the horizon with his eyes closed for a few minutes.

Then he had his left arm straight across his chest and his right hand made this symbol. What was it? It was either a kind of 'C' or an okay symbol? I can't remember. But the right elbow would kind of be at a right angle to the left hand and slowly tilted down. I think it was the opposite for the sun to rise."

Nevaeh rolled her eyes. "It would be awesome if you knew for sure. But whatever."

Noel nudged his sister and gestured at the sun on the horizon. "You gotta try. For Trip."

Nevaeh sighed and faced the west and closed her eyes, taking a few deep breaths. Her eyes snapped open and she did as the duck suggested. As she made a "C" with her right hand, the horizon flashed, colors flooding the sky. Oranges, reds, and pinks all flooded the sky, reflecting against the wispy clouds. The sun moved as her hand did, slowly pulled under the edge of the horizon. She put her hands down and the colors started fading from the sky.

Noel jumped up and hugged her tight. "You did it!"

Nevaeh laughed and danced around with her brother, jumping around. "I did it!"

She turned to Trip and stopped dancing. "Why isn't she moving? We did it, didn't we?"

The duck waddled over to Trip and checked her pulse. "Her heart still beats. I don't know."

Michael hobbled over to Trip, holding her hand tight in his. "Please. Don't leave me now. We did it. We saved this town. The sun set, and the moon rose again. We did it."

Tears started flowing from his eyes as he knelt, brushing his head against hers.

"Please, there has to be something we can do," Noel pled with the duck.

The duck shook her head and said, "I don't know of the moon's ritual. I am sorry."

Noel stamped his foot and stared at the moon rising in the sky. He pointed at it and shouted, "You were supposed to help things! You were supposed to heal. Did I do something wrong?"

Nevaeh walked over, hugging her brother tightly. He buried his head in her shoulder and cried. "I just want everyone to be okay."

Soft light glowed around him as the moon rose higher, flooding the land below with a soft light.

All around, people came back to life again. The fallen animals jerked back to life in Bog, to the tears and hugs of friends who thought them long gone. Blackstone and several citizens of Horizon City opened their eyes again. And finally, Dream Tripper's eyes opened as she gasped for breath.

They all rushed in to hug her and she clung to them. After they finally broke apart, Trip brushed her hand against the crowns on the twin's heads. "I'm sorry you have to bear this burden. I wouldn't have wanted you to pick this up for my sake."

Nevaeh scoffed, crossing her arms. "Burden? Oh please. I got awesome fire powers and we can bring people back to life. What's bad about that?"

Trip opened her mouth but closed it again. She traded a look with Michael who just shrugged. There might be a cost, but it seemed cruel to insist on dampening the twins' mood, if they were coming to terms with their new responsibilities and powers.

Trip smiled and stood up. "Well, we can figure out the details later. I'm just glad you all are okay."

Nevaeh handed Trip her hand back and she screwed it back on with a quick spin.

Blackstone ran up the tower steps and froze as he took in everything he was seeing. "Huh. Well I am certain you four must be tired after such a day. I hope I am not imposing on our new king and queen by offering a place to rest."

Trip and Michael grinned. "That would be great," Trip said. "Thank you."

"I thought we were supposed to be in charge now," Noel pouted, but followed the magician's lead, down the stairs and into the main castle.

They ate good food and celebrated with the citizens for a week solid before Trip pulled Michael aside. "We have to make a decision.

We can stay here with the twins or we can continue on our quest."

Michael sighed and nodded, running a hand through his hair. "I need to keep going. I'm not saying you have to come with me. The twins are safe here and you would be too. You can stay with them."

Trip shook her head, intertwining her fingers in his. "I want to help. I think we all know you'd be dead without help."

He laughed and froze when he saw Nevaeh appear from behind a door. Noel was tugging on her arm but paused when Michael and Trip caught sight of the twins. Nevaeh looked at her brother and then at Michael and said, "That's not the only option."

Noel shook his head, mouthing the words, "No."

But Nevaeh continued, "We have a lot of power now. I think we can create a portal back to your home. You could sleep in your own bed. You wouldn't have to worry about us or the land. Trip can stay here or wander like she likes to."

Michael paused for a moment and then laughed. "I don't want to go home. You guys are my family now. This land is yours and I'm not going to abandon it to whatever fate the gods decide. I have to help. Thank you for the offer, but no."

Nevaeh sprang forward, wrapping her arms around him. He patted her head and said, "I'm not abandoning this place again. I'll stay until the end, no matter what that is."

Trip put her hand on his shoulder and said, "And I'm helping. The twins are safe here and I have to do my part to help the rest of the world."

Noel broke out into sobs, clinging to Michael and Trip. "I'm gonna miss you!"

Trip patted his head and said, "We'll visit. We promise. But we need to go. I love you both."

Blackstone stumbled in and cleared his throat. "I need to borrow the king and queen for their first lessons. They need to learn diplomacy, geography, history. Oh, this will be exciting."

"We will at least be able to learn sword fighting and practice shooting, right?" Neveah asked.

Blackstone shook his head. "You won't need any of those kinds of lessons. You will have soldiers to protect you."

Noel sighed. Trip ruffled his hair and said, "It will be worth it in the end. You will be great leaders."

Nevaeh crashed into her arms and Trip kissed the top of her head. Nevaeh pulled back, tears on her cheeks as she said, "I'm gonna be the best queen ever. So, you better stay safe and come visit."

The twins insisted to load up the golf cart with everything they needed for Michael and Trip's journey. The citizens cheered as they walked down the path out of the town. They waved, but it felt empty.

Trip's smile only fell when they couldn't see the castle anymore. Michael hugged her tight and said, "They will be safer there. They will be okay."

Trip nodded but her voice still shook. "I know. I know. I just can't picture doing this without them. I wish—"

A blue door popped into existence in front of them on the road and Michael slammed on the brakes. The door opened and the twins jumped out, each with a bag of their own.

Nevaeh grinned at the looks on their faces and said, "Did you really think we wouldn't be coming with you?"

Michael shook his head and said, "But what about ruling the kingdom? The rituals?"

Noel shrugged and shoved his bag in the back seat of the golf cart. "Blackstone will take care of the kingdom. He knows more than we do about everything anyways. And we can do the rituals wherever."

Trip opened her mouth and closed it over and over again. "But what about the crowns?"

Nevaeh rolled her eyes and said, "We can make them look however we want."

She clasped hands with her brother and their crowns glowed and shifted, turning into two necklaces. Nevaeh's pendant was still gold and in the shape of a swirled sun while Noel's was silver and the shape of a crescent moon.

Michael glanced over his shoulder back in the direction of Horizon City. "Are you sure you want to come with us? It's going to be dangerous."

Noel grinned and said, "Of course! It'd be boring if it wasn't. Plus, we need each other. Can't lose us that easy."

Unease crossed Nevaeh's features as she said, "Unless you'd rather we didn't come with you?"

Trip opened her arms and hugged the twins tight. "I'd love it if you came."

Michael stood off to the side but was pulled into the hug by Trip. Noel beamed and hugged them both tightly. When he pulled away, he looked up at Michael. "If you don't mind, I'd like to drive."

Michael laughed and waved his hand toward the driver's seat. "All yours."

They piled into the golf cart with a smile and took off.

Michael felt the wind on his face and felt a truth deep in his heart. He was home.

ABOUT THE AUTHOR
George Mendoza

George Mendoza was born in New York City in 1955. At the age of 15, he was diagnosed with a rare, incurable, degenerative eye disease, fundus flavimaculatus. Effects of the disease caused him to lose his central vision, keeping only a gray foggy fringe on the periphery. In the center of his view, he sees what he calls "kaleidoscope eyes"—intense and changing visual images of fiery suns, brightly burning eyes; and colorful pinwheels. These spectacles almost never leave him, not even when he lays down in darkness to go to sleep.

A man of vision and courage, George went on to become a world-class runner and Paralympic contender. In 1980, he broke the world record for blind athletes, running the mile in 4 minutes and 28 seconds. In the early 1990's, he began to paint full-time. Ironically, Mendoza's paintings spring from the loss of his eyesight and a very special vision that took its place. He had grown increasingly frustrated by his dancing colors, which would not leave him alone. He spoke to a priest at the Holy Cross Retreat House in New Mexico. "Paint them," the priest said. "Make designs, pictures from them."

George Mendoza remembers physical sight, and so his works derive from visual memories intertwined with dreams, visions, and emotional experiences, meaning Mendoza paints both figuratively and abstractly. His work then transcends the physical world, exploring the spiritual, the mystical, the playful, and sometimes the darker nuances of the human spirit.

Mendoza works full time as a writer and an artist. Currently, his exhibition "Colors of the Wind" is a national Smithsonian affiliates traveling art exhibit. He lives in Las Cruces, New Mexico, and is founder and president of the Wise Tree Foundation, Inc., a non-profit corporation for the promotion for the arts. He is a motivational speaker and is currently developing a play based on his children's book *Colors of the Wind*, a biography of his life written by J.L. Powers and illustrated using Mendoza's artwork.

Learn more at www.georgemendoza.com.